T0198614

HUNTING GIOVANE

HUNTING GIOVANE

A novel
By Elizabeth Fritz

iUniverse, Inc.
New York Bloomington

Hunting Giovane

iUniverse books may be ordered through booksellers or by contacting:

iUniverse
1663 Liberty Drive
Bloomington, IN 47403
www.iuniverse.com
1-800-Authors (1-800-288-4677)

ISBN: 978-1-4401-6756-0 (pbk)
ISBN: 978-1-4401-6757-7 (ebk)

Printed in the United States of America

iUniverse rev. date: 9/14/2009

Also by Elizabeth Fritz

Surprise! Surprise!
Cousin Delia's Legacy
Hope's Journey
Trio
Assisted Living—or Dying?
Athena

With thanks to

Cheryl and Randy for their unflagging encouragement

✧ 1 ✦

"Madam is not receiving today."

I stood agape, looking up in awe at six feet four of tailcoat and striped trousers. I wasn't accustomed to butlers, much less gigantic ones. The door was closing as I expostulated.

"But I have a letter," I said, scrabbling about in my purse. "I'm requested to present myself at this address at 2 P.M. today. It's signed Agnes DeWitt Emmons."

The lordly being in the doorway extended a hand and taking the now somewhat dog-eared piece of elegant notepaper, glanced at it, opened the door all the way, and gestured me to enter.

"This way," he said, leading me down a majestic hall between magnificently furnished rooms to a small room in the rear: French windows on two sides; white wicker furniture; yellow, white, and green floral chintz, all in all a wonderfully pleasing summer room. Another lordly wave which I assumed was permission to sit down, and he disappeared. I didn't sit down, instead I went to the windows overlooking a vista of yew and box borders around fountains and colorful beds of yellow, pink, and white flowers. A khaki-coated gardener strolled around snipping a twig here and a sprig there with long-handled shears.

"Well, what do you think?"

Startled, I swung around to face the speaker.

"Keeping those parterres manicured must cost a bundle. But it's worth it, I guess."

The old woman standing there snorted, whether in displeasure or agreement, I couldn't tell. She was tall, skinny, very erect, dressed expensively in silvery blue wool crepe, her silver hair coiffed in an elaborate swirl. I knew she was 78 years old (I had done some homework when I received her note) and twice widowed, born to a family of great wealth, and heritor of more millions from each husband. The newspaper photos of her bony, wrinkled face had done her no favors, but cleverly applied makeup softened her appearance in person.

"You're a straightforward young woman. I suppose you disapprove. A lot of people think I should spend my money on the poor instead of elaborate landscaping. Sit down."

"No, ma'am, I don't disapprove. I know you can afford it and that gardener probably supports a family and maybe sends his kids to college on what you pay him. Considering that the garden provides a panorama of great beauty as well, it's all worth it, don't you think?"

"I certainly do think so, or I wouldn't do it. You are not only straightforward, you're brash. Is that how you get results?"

"A little of this, a little of that!"

I wasn't about to back down to this imperious old woman. I wished she would get to the reason she had summoned me. I sat down and prepared to listen; her note had adverted to a "matter of great moment."

I had come out of curiosity. My old friend, Dorset Jones, the curator at the museum, had urged me to accept her invitation, saying "It's likely to be to your advantage, she's richer than Croesus."

Now Mrs. Emmons beckoned me to follow her out of the door to the terrace and to facing marble benches. She sat down opposite me, setting her feet precisely next to one another and smoothing her skirt carefully over her knees. She spent some long moments staring at me. I mustered all the *savoir faire* I could command in order to sustain her close scrutiny without blink or blush. I was glad that in my attempt to appear very businesslike I had put on a shirtwaist dress and low-heeled pumps, a far cry from my usual garb of jeans and tee.

"You don't look old enough for the job but Dorset thought you were right for it. How old are you?"

"Twenty eight, ma'am."

"Married, single, divorced, lesbian?"

"Single, straight." My tone was sharp. What was this old harpy after? I made up my mind to give as good as I got. "Dr. Jones said he had sent you a copy of my *curriculum vitae*. I have to assume you read it."

"Hmm, yes. Well, I'll get to that. You're here because I want you to recover an immensely valuable piece of art removed from my possession some twelve years ago."

"Stolen? What about the police? You certainly understand I am not a private detective."

"It's not a job for a private detective. It wasn't stolen, I loaned it to a dear friend who died with it still in his possession. His heirs have no idea of its value but out of pure spite refuse to return it.

"I don't see how I can help you. You surely have lawyers who can negotiate on your behalf. Maybe they can arrange a financial incentive or a *quid pro quo* of some kind. "

"They've tried those options; I even authorized some discreet blackmail. The heirs remain adamant. I want that piece back and I won't be denied. I want you to find out where and how they are keeping it and how I can retrieve it without publicity. I can make it very much worth your while."

"Worth my while isn't an offer. You're trying to sell me a pig in a poke here. How am I supposed to know whether I want or can do the job for you. You haven't told me enough for me to think I'm qualified for it."

"I'll give you $25,000 up front and expenses to try and another $100,000 if you succeed. *I* think you're qualified and that's all that matters. I won't ask you to do anything illegal or immoral, but if you have to resort to such measures my lawyers will get you off. Well, that's my offer. Are you are willing to gamble on it?"

I made some quick mental calculations. The up front money would pay off the remnant of my student loans and clear the outstanding balance on my car. More importantly it would get me out of my parents' house and into a place of my own. Getting away from Mom and Dad tipped the scale. I took the gamble.

"OK. Now, fill me in."

"Let's walk. It's such a nice day and there will be no eavesdropping in the open air."

❧ 2 ❧

I drove away two hours later mulling over Mrs. Emmons's story while I fought rush hour traffic. Her check was tucked safely in my pocket. Nevertheless, I felt I had to examine the prospects from every aspect. There seemed to be no simple way to attack her problem. After a stop at the night depository of the bank I arrived home and parked at the curb in front of the house. Dad's car, exercising and emphasizing his right as paterfamilias, stood in the one-car garage, Peter's clunker squatted in the drive. Low man on the totem pole parked in the street. Dad had recently retired and now moped grim and glum while sitting on a porch chair all day long in good weather, an occupation interrupted only by an occasional trip to take Mom to the grocery. He nodded as I crossed the porch. Peter sprawled his 350 pounds over the sofa in front of the TV in the living room; he grunted as I passed by. Peter was my brother, older by seven years. On his first and only job, he had suffered an injury that won him perpetual disability payments and eternal leisure time. He was demolishing a bag of potato chips as he watched Judge Judy dispense justice to two sisters quarreling over which would pay the vet bill for spaying their cat. Mom was stirring something oniony in an aura of cooked cauliflower or maybe it was broccoli. Briefly I felt pity for the drabness of her life and looks; Dad and Peter were not easy to live with which was why I spent an absolute bare minimum of time in this house. I graduated high school one day and the next Dad told me I'd better get a job because he was done supporting me. Furthermore, if I stayed on in his house I would owe him $100 a month for board, room, and laundry. By careful management I was able to eat most of my meals elsewhere. There was no joy to be had anyway at the gloomy table with Peter gobbling, Dad grumbling, and Mom whining.

I got jobs right away: McDonald's at the grill on the morning shift, and another as a gofer afternoons and evenings at McKee Graphics. McKee's was a sophisticated operation catering to corporations committed to classy advertising. I sandwiched in classes at the Community College and by diligent application achieved a B.A. in three years. In my final year, trading on my experience with McKee and a friendship I had struck up with Dr. Dorset Jones, I won a scholarship to the graduate program in Fine Arts at the University. Working full time at McKee and part-time for Dr. Jones at the U kept me out of the Crenshaw house and household from "kin see to cain't." No one missed me and I went my solitary way without interference from the family. Dr. Jones quickly became Jonesy as our friendship grew and ripened. Jonesy was short, fat, bald, red-faced, probably gay, in his 60s, and he undertook to teach me what Fine Arts were. For him, they were an obsession. He was a tenured professor at the U with the additional responsibility of curator of University Museum's art collections. His abiding goal was to build the collections by adding rare and splendid items at bargain prices. He hated to travel and often sent me as his deputy to evaluate and negotiate for pieces he had heard of. McKee had finally rebelled at my frequent absences. Our parting was pleasant but definitive. But I had achieved my M.F.A. and Jonesy had come up with a grant from the Torgerson Foundation that paid a reasonably decent no-frills salary. I loved my job; I practically lived at the Museum; and I tackled every search and rescue assignment that Jonesy gave me with energy and joy. Among my recent successes were the acquisition of an exquisitely carved ivory crucifix, Coptic, 8th century in a gold frame; a rare manuscript of the Gospel of Mark, patiently illuminated by an Irish monk in an ancient monastery, still undated but likely 800 years old; and a charming miniature painted on ivory by Thomas Jefferson's great good friend Maria Cosway and thought to portray his mulatto daughter at a very early age. These successes probably fueled Jonesy's recommendation of me to Mrs. Emmons.

"Zima, your mail's on the washer beside your clean laundry. Have you had your supper? I can put on an extra chop." Mom's interest in my dinner as usual lacked enthusiasm.

"No, thanks," I said. "I'm going back to the Museum. I'll get something at the Student Commons."

I went up to my room, changed to jeans and a sweat shirt, and flipped through the mail: two art catalogs, an overstock catalog from Lands' End, my bank statement and credit card bill. Before leaving for the U I looked around at the room, identifying possessions I had acquired with my own money. I would have to take a furnished apartment, even the bed and desk were hand-me-downs purchased originally for Peter's room. Moving would amount to no more than packing a couple of suitcases and some cardboard boxes and taking down some framed prints and posters. My books and laptop were in my cubbyhole office at the Museum.

On my way out, Mom breathed a languid bye-bye, Peter grunted again, and Dad woke from his doze long enough to lift his hand in a weak gesture of farewell. As I swung my rattletrap VW into the side street that ran along one side of the campus, I saw a **ROOMS FOR RENT** sign in the window of one of the huge old Victorian mansions that lined the street. I stopped and talked with a frail white-haired woman, viewed a one-bedroom efficiency that, among others, had been carved out of the former ballroom, and came out with a key and a copy of a signed lease. When I had commented on the grubby state of the apartment and the beat up furniture, Mrs. Puckett apologized at some length—students are so careless, you know—but she hastened to emphasize that the price was right. And she recommended Ms. Shafer, another tenant, a student who supported herself by cleaning and painting, very reasonable. I should just think of the convenience of the Wash-A-Way Laundromat located around the corner within walking distance. I could move in as soon as my deposit and first month's rent check cleared. I braced myself for Dad's reaction to my announcement of departure. A few years ago, Dad had raised my contribution to the Crenshaw household finances to $150 a month. He would throw a fit over losing it. So be it!

3

Reaching my office I pulled a notepad out of my purse and sat down to ponder the scribbles made while jogging along beside Mrs. Emmons on our garden walk. I decided to write up my notes more or less formally on the laptop, both to get the facts organized and to identify questions for which I still needed answers. I remembered a remarkable amount of her verbal information. She was a colorful teller of memorable tales. This is what I wrote:

> Agnes Cathcart DeWitt Emmons. Born to great
> wealth, reared in luxury. Cathcart patents for plumbing
> equipment very lucrative. Lived in France with parents
> until World War II. With U.S. entry into the war
> imminent, father packed up their large collection of
> Renaissance and Impressionist art, sailed on one of the
> last liners to make a peacetime crossing of the Atlantic.
> Married at 18 to William Henry DeWitt, DeWitt
> automotive fortunes. Cathcart art collections ended up in

DeWitt and later Emmons estates. DeWitts shared love
of collecting.

[My comment: Agnes's love and lifelong knowledge of art, learned
in childhood, continued into maturity. Probable source of her passion
to recover the lost piece of art—the source but not entirely the reason,
as I was to learn.]

Agnes madly in love with W.H. DeWitt until he died
when she was in her 40s. Agnes then lived absolutely
conventionally for 10 years, committed to social causes
and good works. With a wry smile, she confessed to
taking advantage of the relaxed social atmosphere of the
1970s, enthusiastically adopting women's liberation.
Deliberately shed her bras. Eschewed contraceptive
devices (which Mother Nature had obviated anyway).
Appeared in public in two-piece bikinis. Dumped all
the hypocritical standards of her class and upbringing.
Discreet love affairs with a number of highly satisfactory
sexual partners. 'I was careful never to trespass on
another woman's territory,' she laughed, 'women make
good friends but bad enemies.' A stable of lawyers and
a modicum of prudence kept her amours out of the
newspapers. Married Walter Anderson Emmons, 'On
impulse, the very worst reason to marry, don't you ever
do it,' she cautioned. Marriage to Walter was OK, he was
filthy rich and very indulgent, but in the event deathly
boring, especially since his sex drive bordered on zero.
In years to come, Walter so fascinated by fashionable
ailments, by medications, by doctors, by drug and diet
regimens, convinced himself his health was precarious.
'What's that proverb that the thought is father to the

deed?' Patronized spas and health clinics. Dwelt endlessly
on his health problems. Bored Agnes, bored their friends,
bored his business associates, bored his bankers. Agnes
escaped to the villa in Antibes. Took up with a beautiful
bronzed Adonis, whose *métier* was sailing expensive
yachts for rich people too inept to sail on their own.
Agnes had no illusions. Knew it wouldn't last but enjoyed
his favors until a more generous woman outbid her and
he drifted away. That was about 15 years ago.

[This is where her story grew interesting, to me, that is. So far she
had related the adventures of a spoiled child and a willful woman,
too rich and too undisciplined to practice moderation, whether it
was spending money or playing at relationships. I found it hard to
sympathize with her self-absorption and ingrained selfishness. But
she was paying me for action not sympathy. I couldn't help thinking
her biography would make a best-selling popular novel; I envisioned
a paperback with a lurid cover. I had to admire her lawyers; she was
never in a tabloid that I ever saw.]

At loose ends after Adonis whose true name was
Giovanni, she traveled around European capitals,
haunting art dealers, looking for bargains to fill gaps in
her collection of 17th century woodcuts. In Paris still
smarting a bit from the desertion of her Adonis, she
spotted a small painting attributed by its provenance
to the 'school of Rembrandt.' Probably a study for
something larger, just a portrait face in three-quarters
profile, a young man's face like enough to her Adonis that
she coveted it for a memento. Thorough investigation
authenticated original record of purchase and possession
by four generations of a noble French family that had

emigrated to escape the Revolution. As émigrés the
family forfeited its *biens** to the egalitarian government
which sold them off to prosperous farmers. Contents of
a chateau got stowed away in the attic of a farmhouse.
Paintings found after World War I among a bunch
of others were sold to an art dealer, sold, and resold,
growing dirtier and smudgier with each transfer. When
the piece resembling her ex-lover captured her fancy, she
paid $20,000 for it. Took it to an expert restorer who
called her in a state of high excitement when under the
grime he found a flourish, R.v.R, Rembrandt's own mark.
Not just 'school of Rembrandt' the master himself. From
$20,000 the value of the painting had skyrocketed to two
million.

[Agnes was ecstatic then and still; not only had she satisfied
sentiment for an ex-lover and perhaps taken a small revenge for his
desertion, she had got a fantastic work of art at an incredible bargain.
I began to appreciate that possessing was her obsession; she did not
intend to suffer lightly loss of her prize.]

Purchases from her European buying tour went home
to the Emmons house. She hung the painting in her
bedroom. 'I liked to look at it, I considered it a trophy
twice maybe three times over.' She named it Giovanni in
fond remembrance of her Italian Adonis.

Walter Emmons soon preoccupied himself into an
early grave. 'No great loss,' Agnes said without a trace of
regret, 'he was as good as dead anyway.' Agnes resumed
free-wheeling easy-come, easy-go affairs, until she met
and fell head over heels for Adrian Cash. Bubbling

* Wealth, property

with enthusiasm she described him, 'A genuine matinee idol, but you're too young to remember him. He was incredibly handsome, incredibly debonair, and an incredibly exciting lover.'

[I had heard of him as an antediluvian survivor of the era of the epics of my childhood. I had even seen him on the screen: a bare-chested, muscle-bound barbarian in a fur loincloth, brandishing a sword, or maybe a spear. By the time she fell in love with him, he hadn't had a starring role in years. But for an Agnes Emmons, a matinee idol was a matinee idol. I felt a transient pang of pity for her. Her fascination with Cash seemed authentic and unalloyed. For all Agnes's selfishness, she had a hard core of common sense and a flair for absolute honesty in describing her adventures. She went on with her story, her eyes misty with remembered gratification. As her delivery of the facts grew more fluent, my notes took on the style of a real narrative and I realized I had almost total recall of her conversation.]

She and Cash most often made love in her bedroom in the Emmons mansion under the gaze of the Rembrandt painting. Adrian, she said, was rather jealous of the attachment she displayed for it, not her attachment to the painting but to its resemblance to her Adonis. She teased him saying he had to exert himself to measure up to the brio of her bronzed sailor. Finally, Cash was irritated enough to bet her he could give her a marathon of sexual pleasure that would relegate the memory of Giovanni to the back burner for all time. Agnes simpered as she recalled that over a 24-hour period he had won the bet hands down and claimed as his prize the painting of his rival. She refused to give it to him but offered to loan it to decorate his bedroom, motivation for stellar performance on home ground on those occasions when they made love there. The painting was so much a subject of banter that one day when she visited him she found he had inserted an autographed studio photo of himself into the frame over the canvas. Beneath it he had pinned a card reading NOW WHO'S NUMBER ONE? She had laughed until the tears came.

The affair with Cash came to an end while she was on a trip to Florida. She had gone with friends on a three-week cruise, out of touch with mainland news. In the interim Cash who was deep in debt (living as an aging gigolo was not particularly remunerative) suffered a mortal cardiac event. His creditors jumped on his belongings like ducks on June bugs. Everything was attached for sale as movie memorabilia, the masked Rembrandt lost in a pile of photos of Adrian's old friends from the movie community. Agnes was so upset by Adrian's death, she suffered a mini-stroke, what doctors call a TIA. It was weeks before she remembered the Rembrandt and put the detective from the insurance company on its trail. By then the trail was cold. That's how the Rembrandt got out of her hands and the Rembrandt was what she wanted me to get back.

$\eateq 4 \eateq$

"Why now?" I had asked. "Didn't you say the painting disappeared some 12 years ago?. Have you had some news of it since? A ransom demand, a listing in a gallery catalog?"

"Nothing like that," she said, and went on to relate that the insurance company had lost interest and paid off after seven years without a lead. Recently she had gone with friends to try a new restaurant touted for its retro décor. Framed studio photos of film stars covered the walls above booths where the tables, in the spirit of the recreated time, sported ketchup and steak sauce bottles, hokey salt and pepper shakers, and chrome-plated paper-napkin caddies.

"Slowest service I ever experienced," she said. "nothing to do but wait, put up with scratchy versions of golden oldies playing eternally on a juke box, and look around at the photos. That's when I saw the photo of Adrian in the custom frame I had had built for the Rembrandt."

She said she managed to conceal her excitement but before she left the restaurant she asked the hat check attendant how the photos had been gathered. It appeared that the restaurant owner was Adrian's great-niece. Hooked on the era of the star system of the big studios, she had haunted flea markets and sidewalk sales collecting photos to decorate her period establishment. Betty Cash was reported to have practically danced in the streets when she came across the photo of her relative.

"What made you think it was still the masked Rembrandt? Just the frame?"

No, not just the frame. That had been painted to match the décor, but it had retained its unusual size and style. Agnes had promptly hired a private detective to pose as an appraiser for Betty Cash's insurance company. His inspection included looking at the back of each of the photos. He reported that he saw behind the frame of Adrian's photo something that looked like wood strips with canvas stretched over them. Agnes immediately approached Betty Cash begging to buy it. "I told her of my liaison with Adrian and how meaningful that photo was to me. I offered her $300 for it because I didn't want her to think it was valuable. I added some sentimental tears to my story but I must have laid it on too thick. She grew suspicious and refused me across the board. She insisted the photo was more meaningful to her because Adrian was her only famous relative and she meant to keep it. I tried to buy it more than once, escalated the offer to $600 in the end. The last time I went by the restaurant the photo was gone, put away she said to get me out of her hair. I sent the detective to find out where it was now but he came up dry."

"How long ago was this?" I asked.

"Last June. I put the detective on watch for news of it. A month ago I heard that Betty's restaurant venture had gone belly up; the Cashes seem to have trouble with cash flow," she giggled over her rather lame witticism. "Anyway, I disguised myself and went to the sheriff's sale of her belongings. The picture wasn't among the personal and business items on the block. I'm disillusioned with that detective; I'm not even sure he's still trying and I know he wouldn't know the Rembrandt if it bit him in the butt. I read how you found the crucifix and negotiated its acquisition for the Museum, so I called Dorset Jones to get your address. I bribed him with a promise to display the Rembrandt in the Museum if you were to recover it."

The information Agnes provided to me was so extensive that I felt I could plan initial search efforts with only a few more questions of her. She would have to release to me the insurance company's undoubtedly detailed description of the painting; I hoped there would be a photograph of it. I would have to roam the public displays of movie memorabilia. I did not expect to find Adrian's photo so much as to get a feeling for the kind of people or institutions that collected such stuff. Although collectors and collections of classic art work were familiar to me, movie buffs and their stuff were not. I wanted to talk with the detectives she had hired or get copies of their written reports (if such existed). No need to plow new ground for hints or unrecognized clues. I made lists and notes until I suddenly realized it was long past midnight. The broken-down sofa in my office became my bed for the night, as it had so many times when I was preparing a hunting expedition. I was short but it was shorter so I expected to be aching when I woke up.

The next morning I was washing up in the Museum rest room when I heard Jonesy's halloos in the hall. When I popped out to greet him, he began, "I wish you'd carry your cell phone. You weren't home last night and the phones here were shut down. I wanted to tell you Agnes Emmons had talked to me after you left. She told me I was right; you were right for her project." His eyes glistened with greed as he added, "Wow, Oh Wow! Can't you just see that Rembrandt hanging in the Dutch Masters Room?"

17

"We don't have a Dutch Masters Room."

"We will. Just you get that Rembrandt and we will. Emmons money will build and start to furnish it."

I had to chuckle, his enthusiasm was as energetic as it was premature.

"Did Agnes tell you how the painting got away from her?"

"Sketchy, got something to do with a studio photograph of Adrian Cash. I was something of a fan of his before his butt caved in and his belly bulged. Made a hell of a naked hero in his salad days."

"The photograph is the clue I have to pursue first. Who do you know that collects or displays movie memorabilia? I'd like you to issue some introductions and bona fides for me."

Jonesy repaired to his office and emerged an hour later with a list.

"Check marks mean I've called already and you're welcome. No check marks, ask them to call me; they're the collectors who play close to their vests. I made up a story that I'm thinking of an exhibit and you are scouting for material."

"You continually amaze me. I never suspected you had so many contacts in that milieu. Or were such a facile liar."

"Movies are one of the Fine Arts and the people who figure in them have the Oscars to prove it. Don't sell them short. This will be a learning experience for you and who knows, I may make that lie come true, depending on how well you learn the lesson. If I do, I'll put a sign over it MOUNTED BY ZIMA CRENSHAW. You will have made your bones without bloodshed."

I laughed, never dreaming there would literally be bloodshed in the future.

❧ 5 ❧

My first order of business was to get myself out of my parents' house. I finished up a few odds and ends on my desk, picked up some empty boxes at the liquor store, and went home. I packed my luggage and the boxes and began carrying them down to my car. My first trip interested no one, the second drew raised eyebrows from Peter and a puzzled look from Mom, the third and last immediately preceded my announcement to Dad that I was leaving for good. As expected, he exploded. He rose from his chair waving his arms and shouting.

Incredibly, when he ran out of breath, I managed to get in the last word. "You don't have to refund the balance on my last month's board and room. Here's my new address. I'll notify the Post Office. Good-bye."

As I drove away Mom was standing on the porch, her face puzzled and woeful, twisting the scrap of paper with my new address between shaking hands. Deep down, I felt sorry.

Mrs. Puckett had called the bank twice, once in the morning before my check was posted to my account, and again in the afternoon after it was posted. So when I arrived in the late afternoon, she greeted me at the door with a smile. I looked up Ms. Shafer immediately and engaged her services.

"Give me a week," she promised, "and you won't know the place. I need 20 bucks for paint and another 20 for first-time cleaning. What color do you want? Only one to a customer. I'll start as soon as I have your money. I collect three dollars a week per user for keeping up the bathroom."

I ate dinner at the Student Commons, then spent the evening at Walmart picking up linens and kitchen utensils. The apartment boasted a minuscule sink, a two-burner hot plate, and a 4.5 cubic foot refrigerator. The bed at Puckett Hall was even worse than my office sofa; the mattress was monumentally lumpy and its middle sagged almost to the floor. It was somewhat improved when I found three slats nailed up in an alcove for shelves and reinstalled them under the springs. The communal bathroom was sparkling clean, thanks to Ms. Shafer's attentions. Contributions collected from users went to pay her rent. A schedule hung on the bathroom door; Apartment 2A (mine) was allowed 30 minutes at 7 A.M. and at 9 P.M. for showering, no laundering permitted. A note appended to the schedule indicated that additional and/or different times were negotiable, see Ms. Shafer.

Ms. Shafer was emerging as a woman of parts. She was about 23, working on a degree in elementary education, some 24 credits yet to go. Coffee with cream complexion, sparkling black eyes, hair in corn rows, elegant figure (she said she sometimes modeled for a local department store), mind like a steel trap. So far she said proudly, she had maintained a 3.6 GPA, and she planned to parlay it into a Master's degree if everything went right. I would take bets that things would go right for her; she was determined and capable and not afraid to work to get to her goal. When she finished with the apartment, walls, cupboards inside and out, floor, and desk, table, and chairs were pale blue. I floated around in my monochrome ambience like a satisfied butterfly. Ms. Shafer, whose Christian(?) name was Zulu, had found an antique pier glass in the Puckett basement, borrowed it from Mrs. Puckett, and carried it up it for me. I inaugurated it by standing in front of it and examining myself.

Top to toe, I hit 5 feet 4. Slicked down black bangs hung down to unruly black eyebrows over bright blue eyes and ruddy cheeks—far from pretty, but fair enough to have attracted some romantic fellows for whom I had never had time. Wow, could I ever empathize with Zulu; both of us could claim our educations hard-won. Pity that Horatio Alger hadn't heard of us or hadn't had the social conscience to write up women who showed PLUCK and hoped for LUCK. I considered the pier glass a start on the luck. Assuring that my blouse was tucked in and my panty hose were taut had become important since I needed to present myself in stylish garb to the institutional staffs and often very wealthy collectors that I was contacting.

We women weren't the only ones struggling to get through our educations. Juan Carrizozo lived in another unit on the second floor. He was working on a degree in astrophysics and on the side for Mrs. Puckett doing minor repairs and lawn care. English as a second language was not easy for him, and he was bitterly discouraged as his major professor kept making him rewrite and rewrite his thesis. I didn't know beeswax about astrophysics but I offered to help him with grammar, spelling, and syntax if he would make some of those minor repairs in my apartment. Amazingly, I learned something about the topic from the editing I did and after the next submission, Juan qualified for his orals. His dark face beamed in puppy dog gratitude as he told me of his success and I was blessed with cupboard doors that latched and proper shelves in that alcove. Zulu, Juan, and I celebrated with a pizza bash.

ॐ 6 ॐ

While Zulu was working on the apartment, I was beginning my calls on the institutions and people on Jonesy's list. My ploy when viewing a collection was to compliment the collection or collector in glowing terms, then to get him or her talking (never difficult) about the items and the vicissitudes of collecting them, and finally to introduce a low-key mention of Adrian Cash into the conversation. I often found the personalities more intriguing than the collections. There was, for instance, an amiable young man named Hillis Brennan, the delightfully quirky curator of a private museum called Movie Moments. He was a hunchback, diminutive, his back and neck warped into an S-shape that forced the gaze of his bent head to look over his left shoulder at a 45 degree angle from his body. He scuttled crabwise as he walked me through the displays. When we talked, he sat on a tall stool and looked down on me sitting in a chair. His scintillating personality completely distracted me from his deformity but left me curious as to the origin of his name. He explained,

"I was christened George Alexander and accounted a beautiful baby. But after infancy, this scoliosis developed and progressed. The doctors declared it impossible to correct so I and my family learned to live with it. Disability allowed me to immerse myself in a myriad of wonderful worlds of books, music, and movies. When I was sixteen, I happened on a poem that began, 'No hill is too high to climb.' I took it for my life's motto and got the court to change my name to Hillis."

Guts, I thought, unbelievable guts. Talk about turning a lemon into lemonade. Hillis's special expertise lay in posters that studios used to provide for the glass cases on the fronts of movie houses. He presided over rows of swinging racks holding hundreds of these brightly colored, often lurid pieces. The pictorial work ranged from the utterly tasteless to quality worthy of a Rembrandt exhibit but only one item featured Adrian Cash. It advertised *The Way of The Flesh,* a T&A* epic that Hillis dismissed as having no redeeming social value. He valued it, however, because the artist was Lili Cohn.

"She was one of the best," he said, "but her work is very scarce. I don't really know why. You might want to look her up, she's still alive. If she talks to you, try to find out why there're so few posters of hers around."

I decided to follow up on Lili Cohn. I found her in a wheelchair in a nursing home, feisty at 88, more than willing to talk about her old job at MGM. She peered up from under a mop of orange hair (her own, to judge from the snow-white roots), eyes twinkling in her wrinkled face. She wore orange lipstick badly applied to her lips and smeared on her dentures. I told her I had seen *The Way of The Flesh* poster and that Hillis wondered why there were so few Lili Cohns available to be collected.

"Well," she snapped, "the studio claimed ownership of everything

*Slang for Tits and Ass, depictions that in Rembrandt's day were fine art.

I did. So they've got stacks and stacks of originals squirreled away somewhere, damp, rat-chewed, moldering, you can bet. I did sneak out a few, you'll laugh when I tell you how. There was a time when dirndl skirts were a fad, and I would wrap a poster original around my hips before I walked off the lot. All them gathers covered up the bulge but I had to fold 'em and nowadays you can tell most of the genuine Lili Cohns by the crease. I figured I had a right. There were a couple that didn't have a crease, I rolled 'em up and carried 'em bare faced past the gate guard when he wasn't real alert. I didn't sell them then, just hung them on the wall in my bedroom, but when times got hard for me, I got enough from them to keep me in this snake pit until I die."

"Did Adrian Cash pose for you, or did you paint him from a still?"

"Pose!" she snorted, "You betcha! Could hardly get the paint on the canvas. Most of the time that rag around his hips was off and we was rollin' around on the floor, makin' out." A nostalgic sigh. "He was a better lover than an actor; too bad, he died young, compared to me that is."

"I heard he had a lot of movie memorabilia that got sold up when he died. Did you ever hear anything about that?"

"No, I couldn't get to the auction, although I heard it barely brought enough to pay his debts. Some rich woman was keepin' him but he liked to live high and what she doled out wasn't enough to support the life style he favored outside of her bedroom. Say, honey, if you are interested in Adrian Cash, go see his daughter. Her name is Glenda Carter. I used to have her address but it got lost somewhere along the way. She might be in the phone book, she lived in a little town in the boondocks, Siena, Senna, Senta, something like that. Iced cakes for a living."

I bid Lili farewell, promising to drop in again for more stories of the old days.

"Lord willin,' I'll be here!" she caroled.

Lili was another keeper for *my* collection of outstanding personalities. I didn't get to Glenda Carter right away but I did find an address and phone number for a G Carter in a phone book for the town of Sierra. I suspected she was related to Betty Cash, an aunt perhaps. My next contact was Harry Western, a former magnate of an obscure studio that had been bought out by Desilu. Western was a recluse, but Jonesy's name was a magic key to his vast wrought iron gates and majestic marble portal. I was met by an Asian houseman and led to a seat in a magnificent drawing room furnished entirely in Louis XVI gilded wood and white silk damask. I recognized a Monet, a Pissarro, a Corot, and a Murillo hanging on the walls. I knew of the Murillo as one with a murky reputation but Mr. Western wouldn't be the first rich collector to be fooled by a fake. What surprised me was the décor. Considering that Western's reputation was for his collection of props used in famous movies, 18th century French furniture and Impressionist masterpieces were unexpected.

The soft-footed houseman returned to usher me down a staircase to a windowless underground anteroom where Harry Western was awaiting me. The door leading from the anteroom resembled the entry to a bank vault, combination lock and all. After a muffled greeting, Mr. Western turned to the lock and carefully hiding his manipulations with his body, twirled the dial. Western was dressed in riding breeches and a tweed jacket; I was reminded of the old photos of directors in boots on location and waving a megaphone. By golly, he *was* wearing boots; this was a collector bent on playing a part. We went through the open door that Western cautiously closed behind us into a huge hall, one end of which was a fully furnished movie theater with an enormous screen behind the drapery of a gold-fringed velvet curtain. The ranks of chairs were upholstered in authentic cut velvet. An odor of freshly made popcorn pervaded the air. When I commented, Mr. Western mumbled that there was an additive to the air handling system that created the odor when he admitted guests to the hall.

I stood amazed as lights flashed on in glass cases lined up on one of the walls. There were also free-standing etageres encased in glass. I drew a deep breath, the display was so splendid. Mr. Western was so pleased with my reaction, he took my hand to lead me to his favorites.

"This is one of the pairs of ruby slippers made for *The Wizard of Oz,"* he said. "Aren't they beautiful? And over here is the costume of the Munchkin mayor who greeted Dorothy."

Opening a door to a side hall, he towed me around a classic car, WW I vintage, perfectly restored.

"Clifton Webb took the family driving in the original *Cheaper by the Dozen*. Myrna Loy sat right here." He pointed to the passenger seat and sighed, "Now, she was a star to remember."

Our next stop was a display of guns, antiques that had been copied for a dozen or more famous western movies and carried by the likes of Henry Fonda, Gary Cooper, Clark Gable, and Jimmy Stewart.

"These are the originals, you see. Too valuable for actual use. The stars brandished and fired replicas, especially made in the studio workshops."

I found it difficult to change the subject to movie personalities. With the exception of Myrna Loy, Western's horizon began and ended with the *things* that had figured in important movies, many of them made without his involvement. I wondered how he had made the fortune that obviously supported his life style and obsession with props. Later

I learned from Jonesy, he had married a famous producer's daughter and inherited from him through her. Finally, I got in a question about Adrian Cash.

"Did you have anything from an Adrian Cash movie? I'm interested in the memorabilia that was dispersed after his death. Writing a book, you know, about the period of his heyday."

"Nothing here," he answered grumpily. "Cash was never my idea of a star. I went to the auction of his stuff but the only thing I looked at was a serape he was supposed to have worn as an extra in *Treasure of the Sierra Madre*. But when I looked at it, it had a label 'made in Japan' and I had no use for trash."

"I'm interested particularly in a studio photo portrait of him in a rather elaborate frame. Did you happen to notice something like that at the auction? One of my sources is trying to run it down."

"I wasn't looking at anything like that, although I did notice a woman in a red hat who bid for it. Looked like a chippy but that was his style."

"Was her bidding successful?" I ventured. A female admirer acquiring this photo would be quite a good lead.

"Don't know, don't care. Now, over here I've got …," and he led me off to another case, this one displaying Victorian oil lamps from the original make of *Meet Me in Saint Louis*. I finally escaped, pleading an appointment elsewhere. I intended to look up the auctioneer or auction house that had handled the Cash sale; perhaps I could get a name for the woman in the red hat. One thing I did NOT do was add Harry Western to my list of outstanding personalities. His tunnel vision disqualified him.

❧ 7 ❧

One day I came home, my feet aching from a day of fruitless prowling in photo galleries, and met Mrs. Puckett at the door with a fat manila envelope from Agnes Emmons in her hand. The envelope contained the insurance record for the Rembrandt and reports filed by the detectives who had searched for it. I was tired and loath to concentrate on the contents as intently as I knew I ought. I told myself that after a good night's sleep, my mind would be sharp and receptive to nuance. I decided to take the envelope to my office at the Museum in the morning. For now I only leafed through the papers, although I spent a few minutes captivated by the photo of the Rembrandt. I could see why Agnes was so taken by it; it was not only a splendid example of Rembrandt's work, but the portrait face was beautiful in its youthful masculinity and haunting in its romantic pose and color qualities. I returned it to the envelope but having seen that face, I felt a curious responsibility for safe storage of the envelope. I had no reason to worry, only Mrs. Puckett had seen the envelope and its return address, and my disquiet was nothing but moon dust, but I nevertheless judged the

Museum building's security by far superior to the shaky lock on my apartment door. Forgoing a shower in the bathroom, in a three minute visit I accomplished only the essential and then did a spit wash in my sink.

My night was a restless one; a new crop of lumps had surfaced in the mattress and no amount of wriggling could avoid them. And when I dozed, I dreamed. The sidelong glance of the man in the portrait loomed up over and over in the darkness of my mind—teasing, promising an indefinable something. I saw the day dawn through my single window and couldn't go back to sleep. So I did another spit wash (Zulu frowned on ad lib showering, too much noise outside of posted hours), dressed, and went to the office. Vic, the night guard, left me in after some token grumbling, and I went right to work.

I began with the insurance documents since they summarized the provenance of the painting. Gauthier, Comte DuManoir, had commissioned a portrait of his heir, Gauthier II; his letter ordering the portrait required submission of a sample from Rembrandt and Agnes's painting was the sample. The count apparently did not follow through to a full size portrait. I wondered why. Cash flow problems? Gauthier II fallen from paternal favor? Whatever, the painting was listed in the inventory of Gauthier II's property and subsequently in Gauthier III's. The next listing was in the inventories prepared by a notary when the DuManoir properties were confiscated and the contents of the chateau were sold. The contents of the chateau included several paintings (among them the Rembrandt) and became the property of Jacques Bouvier, *fermier**. The next record was a photostat of a letter written by an American GI to his sister in New Jersey. Willie Duncan related how he and his platoon had taken refuge in an unoccupied stone farmhouse near Mortagne to fight off a bunch of Jerries. The attic was full of stuff

---

* Farmer

that Willie and his buddy liberated and sold to a no doubt secretly gleeful junk dealer in Paris for 400 francs, enough for a victory blast. The paintings passed from dealer to dealer for the next 20 years until the painting came to be labeled "Giovane vestiti Cappella,* school of Rembrandt," and ended up in the hands of the dealer from whom Agnes had purchased it. There was no explanation how the painting had acquired an Italian name. The final documents of the provenance were the bill of sale and letters from three world-renowned art experts declaring it a Rembrandt from the hand of the master himself. Another letter from a Sotheby's appraiser quoted a guesstimate of at least $2,000,000 if sold at auction. The insurance company wrote the policy for that amount.

The quality of the photograph was excellent. The long tail of the hat (in exact terms a tippet) richly crimson with a narrow fur band, every hair distinct, draped over Gauthier's right shoulder and a smooth fall of golden hair, highlighting a creamy shirt collar. I smiled as I realized I had put myself on first name terms with the young man. To me he was Giovane.** But, that face, that expression, the trace of mockery in his eyes, the tantalizing twist of his full lips, irresistible! The painting had been photographed on its original wood, placed on a measuring grid; it was 17 inches tall and 8 ¾ inches wide, good size for an exemplar. A second photograph showed the painting mounted in its custom frame, four inches wide, flared and grooved, teak in a dark finish. In order to insert a photo to cover Gauthier's disturbing image, Adrian Cash had to obtain a custom photograph of an unusual size. I wondered if there was a record of Cash's special order among photographers catering to movie personalities some 12 years ago.

Detectives' reports made dull reading after the exotic details of

---

*Young man in a hat
**Pronounced as Joe-Von

the history of the painting. The detective assigned by the insurance company 12 years ago was named William Brady; his report was literate and detailed but not particularly informative. For some reason, he had never pursued the obvious trail implied by Adrian Cash's photograph. He had concentrated on interviews with art dealers, museum curators, and collectors known for their interest in Dutch painters. I wondered if he had worked only from the insurance company's record, ignorant of or ignoring the role of the photograph as memorabilia concealing the painting. In any case, going back to the sources he chronicled was unlikely to generate much in the way of clues. I made a note of his address and tried to phone for a personal interview but reached only his widow. She was his third wife since he had worked for the insurance company; upon his death she had destroyed all of the original notes. Disappointed, I accepted that his written report was the sum and substance of his investigation for all time.

John R. Wicker, the detective Agnes had hired to look at Betty Cash's photo, had taken himself off the case in a letter to Agnes dated only three weeks ago. "Beating a dead horse," were his parting words; he felt he had exhausted all the leads he had turned up. He had included Betty Cash's address and phone number, a brief summary of her past, and a synopsis of the interviews he had with her. I thought a personal interview with Mr. Wicker might be useful, if only to clarify some of the bad grammar and confusing syntax in his report. I took down his address and phone number but decided to get some lunch before I called for an appointment. It was 2 P.M.; I had forgotten to eat breakfast and my stomach was reminding me.

8

When I sat down to my desk again, I added to the original list of people I considered potentially profitable contacts. The list now included Betty Cash, John Wicker, and Glenda Carter. Furthermore I had to run down the woman in the red hat by finding the auctioneer and auction house that handled the sale of Adrian Cash's belongings, and a photographer who made the odd-size print of Adrian's picture. Jonesy was able to furnish the name of three auction houses that handled movie memorabilia. The yellow pages disgorged the names of three photography shops claiming expertise with unusual material. I had some points of departure for continuing my rounds and I hoped for more than sore feet from the searches.

In checking auction houses, I found on my second call the one that had handled the Cash possessions. A very pleasant voice gave me the date and particulars of the "Cash lot" but regretted having no inventory for the lot. House policy destroyed details 10 years after the fact. The auctioneer had been a Claude Zimanski, now retired, but living, I was delighted to find, just two blocks away from my new home. When I called for an appointment a tape announced that Mr. Z was home any time I chose to call. I presented myself at the door of the neat mock-Tudor cottage to encounter a middle-aged, neatly dressed woman. She welcomed me and identified herself as Mr. Zimanski's daughter by means of a buzzer thing she held to her throat. (Jonesy later told me she was probably post-laryngectomy and the appliance allowed her to speak. I told myself I was getting a taste of the real world on this job, meeting real people with real adjustments to life. Twenty eight years as an innocent were coming to an end.) Poppa was in the back garden, she buzzed at me.

Mr. Zimanski must have been in his 80s, still brown-haired and bright-eyed, on his knees in a flower bed, dapper despite a sweater out at the elbows and pants soiled with garden muck.

"Rabbits," he snarled by way of greeting. "Eat every green thing that comes up. I'm trying moth balls as deterrents."

And, indeed a strong odor of naphthalene pervaded the immediate vicinity of a sprinkling of chalky white marbles.

"What can I do for you?" he smiled and stood up. "Randa didn't ask what you wanted, too hard for her to talk on a phone. She just played the tape."

I explained my interest in the auction of the Cash memorabilia and asked if he remembered it. Indeed, he did, remembered every auction he ever called.

"My profession, you see. Doctors remember surgeries, I remember auctions. Adrian Cash's lot wasn't particularly remarkable. Had some rickety furniture, worn carpets, household goods, you know—a lot of photos of himself and of old pals, a handful of almost pornographic charcoal sketches of females, some genuine old vaseline glass, sold the lot for $350."

"Were any pieces sold by themselves?"

"No, bidding was for all or nothing. Which is not to say he hadn't sold off or pawned or bartered some of his stuff in his latter days. He was pretty much on his uppers when he died."

"I heard about a woman in a red hat who showed special interest in a framed photo of Cash himself, rather large, about 24 by 12 inches. A friend has asked me to trace that piece."

Mr. Zimanski shook his head, "I went over that lot myself before it went up, looking for virtu; usually every sell-up has something valuable but unrecognized in it, but the only pieces that qualified were the vaseline glass fruit bowls. Turn of the century stuff, probably his mother's. I remember a woman in a red hat prowling the displays. She seemed to linger longest over Cash's stuff. What I noticed especially about her were the remnants of good looks. I wrote her off as maybe an old flame of Adrian's; he had a lot of them. When she bid, however, it was on a *boule* console table, a replica not worth the seller's reserve, and she didn't persist."

Mr. Z looked up at me, bright as a bird, as I stood there thinking. If the photo wasn't in the stuff up for auction, I wondered where it could have gone in the few weeks after Agnes had last seen it in his apartment and before his belongings went to the auction house. Mr. Z sensed my discouragement, tracing that damn picture was getting ever more complicated. I wasn't sure where I would look next.

"Come on in and have a cuppa coffee. Randa usually has a fresh pot by now."

It would have been churlish to refuse so I joined him and Randa for a pleasant half hour at the kitchen table, not only for fresh coffee but for cinnamon rolls just out of the oven. I left with an invitation to come back any time just to chat.

John Wicker was my next appointment. He received me in his office, a grimy suite in an run-down building in imminent danger of demolition or collapse, whichever came first. He himself was a trim little man, grey, with a Guardsman's mustache and hair cut *en brosse*. I pigeonholed him as a retired military man. He played every card close to the vest and I had to pry every scrap of information out of him. I got him to confirm his report that Betty Cash's picture of Adrian Cash hanging in her restaurant had a wooden inside frame with something like cloth stretched over it. He said Betty had come in while he was inspecting her pictures and raised hell. The insurance company had no business nosing in her business, her premiums were paid up and she had a good clean record with the company. She had obviously said something to catch him on the quick because he was still irritated by her and my next question jolted him into loquacity.

"What made her so mad?"

"She's a born bitch and mad at the world. But maybe I set her off when I said—I was playing my part as an insurance appraiser, you see—the kitchen was a fire waiting to happen. It wasn't more than two weeks before she shut the restaurant down. It must already have been in trouble. And I wouldn't be surprised if she wasn't using something, coke, maybe, or meth."

"I know you had a description of Cash's picture. When you handled it, did anything strike you as odd or different from what you had been told about it?"

"Yes, the outside frame had started out honest brown-varnished teak but she had it painted in red, white and blue stripes to match the décor of her dining room. My hobby is woodworking and it made me mad to see fine wood disfigured like that. Betty and me sure didn't hit it off. When I asked her whether being related to Adrian Cash was how she got such a big picture of him, she nearly took my head off. 'You damn right, I'm related,' she yelled. And then she froze up."

"Why did you resign from the case? Was she that bad? Or did you just run out of questions?"

"A little bit of both. I had reached a point with her where the answer to every question was an obscenity and asking questions was a futile exercise. Besides, I had another job going with far better prospects, both for success and pay. Mrs. Emmons was ragging and nagging me and I just didn't want any more of that either."

He clamped his lips together and I took that for a signal he didn't want any more from me as well. He did give me the last-known address and phone number for Betty Cash; he said he thought she was hiding from creditors, and from him. So I left, more resolved than ever to pursue Betty Cash and Glenda Carter. I had a growing hunch that Betty, Glenda, and Adrian made a triangle with something interesting in common.

❧ 9 ❧

I was sitting at my desk at the Museum, mulling over my current information and moping in discouragement. I didn't seem to be any closer to Giovane than when I started hunting him. What to do next? As I sat there, head in my hands, Jonesy bustled in.

"What's bugging you? Bad luck or no luck at all?" he asked.

I reviewed my recent activities and he spotted my muddle immediately.

"Get back to basics! Betty Cash had the most probable item and had it most recently. I think you been running around wasting energy and time on 12-year-old happenings. Did that ever occur to you?"

His brusque words didn't inspire me as much as they started a new train of thought.

"You know," I said, "I don't even know what Adrian Cash looked like. The only pictures I ever saw of him were Lili Cohn's poster and the movie I saw when I was 10 years old. Both of those were highly colored depictions, enhanced, larger than life, about as far as they could get from his looks when he played his little joke on Agnes. I wouldn't recognize his picture if it bit me on the nose. Even the frame has been altered, Wicker tells me. Damn it, I wish I could coin a word that summed up that conglomeration: hidden painting slash photograph slash frame. At this moment, I'm not even positive that all three elements are still together."

"Don't swear, it doesn't get you any further. I have a suggestion. Proceed on the assumption that the conglomeration is intact, start calling it the Object, get a copy of **a** photo or ***the*** photo of Cash that is probably part of the Object, look for the Object as a photo in a red, white, and blue frame. Look in the vicinity of Betty Cash or Glenda Carter. How does that sound?"

"It sounds like sense and puts me on the immediate track of the origin of Cash's photo. Next, run down Glenda Carter, I have a notion I can find her fairly easily; then locate Betty Cash whom Wicker hasn't been able to find since she closed her restaurant. Wicker thinks she's hiding from creditors. If the Carter woman is related to her, maybe I can get a line on Betty that way. Thanks, Jonesy, I think I've got my head on straight again."

"That's what friends are for," he said airily and left with a wave and a smile.

I resolved to start calling promising photo shops the next afternoon. I had to get a haircut and do my laundry in the morning. I finished this day's efforts by mining the yellow pages for photo shops and locating the town of Sierra on a state map. I went home and coaxed Juan and Zulu to join me for order-in pizza. We sat at my light blue table on my two light blue chairs and Zulu's step stool and put the cares of our respective lives behind us with a bucket of beer and casual conversation.

The evening was a pleasant interlude for me and I suspected for them as well.

The hair stylist talked me out of bangs and into a gamine cut the next morning. I barely recognized myself with feathers of hair sticking out all over my head but on mature consideration decided I rather liked it. One thing about changing hair styles: if they're not too radical, they grow out or go away with the next shower. Old Mrs. Delaney, the landlady of the mansion next to the Puckett house, was highly complimentary as we schmoozed over our respective loads at the laundromat. She regaled me with the history of her own hair styles over the past 50 years, from poodle cuts to home perms and most recently to an Afro. Her blue-tinted Afro was quite becoming.

When I got back to the Museum, I felt refreshed and ready to start on my photo shop phone list. Often I had, after running into a dead end on a crossword puzzle, done something else for a while and then gone back to it with relish and rousing success. I wondered if yesterday's seeming dead end was an omen. My second call, to Magella's Picture Place, was a hit: yes, the receptionist treated me to a long tale of her 25-year acquaintance with clients in the movie business, she had autographs from every one; yes, indeed, she remembered when Adrian Cash used to come in for publicity stills…. I interrupted her long enough to learn that they kept every negative on file, you never knew when a star fallen out of favor would come back in a big role, the studios liked to have copies of the old photos in order to restore youthful looks or to soften older ones…. Another interruption allowed me to ask if I might stop by and see the stock of Adrian Cash items.

"Come ahead," she caroled. "We love visitors. Do you have the address? We'll be open till four."

Mrs. Magella, a wispy gray senior citizen, gave me a royal welcome.

She established me in front of a view box with a fat envelope of Cash's negatives organized by date. My chore became so simple I could scarcely believe my good luck. There were only a few negatives from the period 10 to 15 years back. One black-and-white set intrigued me particularly; the pose mimicked Giovane's rather cleverly, suggesting without parodying it. Mrs. M gave me a lens that enlarged and reversed the image of the negative to a print image. I was quietly gleeful; the date and the pose almost assured this as the origin of the photo that Cash placed in the Object. I set Mrs. Magella hunting for Cash's order for the prints made from the negatives of interest; it would undoubtedly specify the size of the print in the Object. She wasn't entirely cheerful about taking on that job. That ancient paper work was buried in dusty old cardboard boxes in the basement but a *pourboire* of $100 sweetened the task. I had an impression that Magella's Picture Place had fallen on hard times; the place was shabby, windows dirty, carpet and upholstery faded. Mrs. Magella seemed to be the only employee on the premises; an extra $100 wouldn't come amiss. While she was looking, I pored over the negatives that I suspected became Cash's joke. Adrian Cash in his 60s was still handsome. Aging flesh had blurred the clean cut planes of his face somewhat but his fine high-bridged nose, broad brow, and sharply defined lips remained arresting. Thick white hair lay in heavy waves over a well-shaped skull. Agnes had said he was incredibly handsome and I could see the justice of her description.

Mrs. Magella returned, her face smudged and hands grubby, carrying an expanding file stuffed with the year's order forms for the negatives I had selected. I was sent to another room to shuffle through them; the precious negatives on the view box had to be preserved from the dust that clung to the papers. The contents of the file were in no order whatsoever, so I had to look at every one until halfway through the pack I came upon one with Adrian Cash's own signature on the form. The sheet enumerated the shots in a set taken 12 years ago and specified an order for a dozen 8 x 10 prints and a custom print, 9 x 18, to be made of shot #8. I asked Mrs. Magella if I could have the order sheet. No, but she would make me a Xerox copy.

"Now," I went on, "can you make me a 9 by 18 print of shot #8? I'll pay whatever you charge."

"You must be a big fan! Sure, but we can't make the print in our shop. We'll have to send the job out. It will take at least two weeks and cost a couple of hundred dollars."

When I said cost was no object, she plucked the chosen negative out of the file envelope and put it in a job envelope.

"Maybe you'd like five or six 8 x 10s while you wait for the big one to come back. Mr. Magella can have them ready tomorrow afternoon."

That was an offer I couldn't refuse, those prints would be great for show and tell, so I said great, write it up.

I left the Picture Place walking on air, it didn't take much of a success to lift my spirits. I was sure this was the start of a run of good luck. Glenda Carter, here I come just as soon as I pick up my small photos tomorrow.

❧ 1 0 ❧

I hadn't figured out the approach I would use when I finally found Glenda Carter but I thought about it on my two-hour trip to Sierra. The town was a green oasis in a vast dry valley lying in the folds of a range of low hills. It existed because a heavily-traveled interstate intersected with a state road crossing the hills that gave Sierra its name. It was a pleasant little place. The sign announced a population of 8,500, and the road into town was lined with fast food joints, filling stations, and automobile dealerships. Attractive single-family houses with nicely kept lawns stood on quiet side streets. The downtown sported a county court house of recent vintage and a courthouse square occupied by small businesses: dress shops, a hardware, unpretentious restaurants, the Sierra Times building, and so on. G Carter's address was on a side street; G Carter's phone hadn't answered any of my three tries.

When I stopped at the address and knocked on the front door, an elderly lady deadheading roses in the yard next door called out, "Glenda's not home this time a day. She works at the Kroger out on the south side. But I'll tell you she ain't interested in realtors or insurance salesmen. And neither am I."

I quickly denied any connection with door-to-door solicitation; I told the woman I was gathering information for a book and hoped Ms. Carter would allow an interview.

"Oh, yes, she'd love to tell you about the days she was in the movies. She had some real nice parts and kept some nice momentos. Did you ever see *Flowers of Evil*? That was one she was in, and *Trail to Abilene* was another."

By then, I was edging away to the car, calling out thanks and good bye. The old lady waved her secateurs at me by way of a friendly farewell. The Kroger on the south side was big and new, with a flower shop, bakery, deli, ATM, 1-hour photo service, a pharmacy, bank branch, a coffee bar, the works. It seemed something of an overkill for such a small town but perhaps an unseen hinterland kept it in business. Lili Cohn had said Glenda iced cakes for a living, so I asked for Glenda at the bakery counter. A stout, rosy-cheeked woman directed me to the flower stand.

"Glenda helps out with the flowers after the cake orders is finished. Better hurry, she's off at 2:30."

My tentative inquiry "Ms. Carter?" delivered under a spreading potted palm produced a slender woman clad in an apron. Glenda Carter was still pretty, her skin was barely wrinkled, her short hair was attractively touched with grey, her smile was natural and disclosed excellent teeth. I introduced myself as an aspiring author, and said Lili Cohn had told me Glenda Carter was Adrian Cash's daughter. I spun a yarn about a chapter in progress that needed more background on Adrian, and I hoped she could help me.

She was enthusiastic but…"This isn't a good place to talk. I'll be off duty in 15 minutes and we could go across the street to Higher Grounds and have coffee while we talk. Is that OK? You could go over now and I'll be along very soon."

That sounded like a good plan. She sank into one of the coffee shop's upholstered chairs with a sigh of pleasure, while I brought lattes for the two of us.

"I go in at six," she confided "and today I had a dozen orders for cake. I had to copy a portrait photo for one of them, spent an hour on just that one. Now, what can I tell you about my father?"

I pulled out one of the 8 x 10 prints and gave it to her. I said I hoped to include it in the book. She was speechless with gratitude.

"This is so nice. It looks just like him the last time I saw him, a year or so before I got word he died. I wanted to go to the funeral but my husband at the time wouldn't hear of it. Said sure as death or taxes, somebody would grab on to me to pay his debts. Jimmy had no use for my dad, and I have to admit he had reason. Adrian had borrowed money from me, never paid it back. Jimmy and me were hard up all our married life; we didn't need to cover Adrian's debts. We had enough of our own."

"Tell me about Adrian," I coaxed. "Where was he born and grown up? How did he get his start in movies?"

She began at the beginning. Cash, born Herman Cashman, Peoria, Illinois; quit school at age 16 and ran off to Hollywood; worked as a parking valet at MGM and made acquaintances among people in the movie business. He finally wangled a screen test.

"Oh," Glenda said, admiringly, "he was a fine figure of a man, handsome face and magnificent body. Not much of an actor but after a director labeled him 'highly decorative as long as he kept his mouth shut,' he worked regularly."

At the time Glenda's mother Gina was signed as an ingénue and was consistently employed in some B movie or another, making a pretty decent salary for the time. On her advice Herman changed his name. Adrian Cash's first role was a half-clad barbarian in *Rome,* a potboiler in which he played a gladiator. Because he stripped so well, his roles from then on capitalized on his physique and kept his dialog at a carefully coached minimum. Soon Adrian and Gina were secretly married, working and between them pulling down several hundred dollars a week. As Adrian's acting skills developed, his roles improved and Gina risked a pregnancy; but pregnancy ended her movie career. Glenda was four years old when divorce broke up the family. Glenda was closemouthed about the subsequent years but I detected deep unspoken resentment. I guessed at Glenda's love-hate feelings for her negligent father. Her mother was left with a kid, no job, and inadequate and erratic child support. They moved back with Glenda's grandmother in Sierra and went on welfare.

Adrian dropped out of their lives, but Gina followed his career in the movie magazines. When Glenda was 16, her mother finagled her a few short-lived roles in TV serials and made-for-TV movies. Glenda hated the life; she said the price she had to pay for those acting jobs was too high for her self-respect. I suspected the price fell due on the casting couch. She had married young and often and wasn't proud of her marital record. After Gina and her grandmother had both died and she had split with her third husband, she was grateful still to have the cottage in Sierra.

"I been makin' it out on my own," she said with a gritty smile.

"You said you saw Adrian a year or so before he died. What was he doing then?" I ventured.

"Living off some rich woman, I think. He called up and asked me to meet him at a Starbuck's in Hollywood Acres Mall. Both of us were living in L.A. then and I was curious. I hadn't seen him for years but I had to keep it secret from Jimmy. He said he wanted to see how I was doing, if I was happy, if Jimmy was a good provider. I stopped him right then and there and told him to think of me as a turnip. If he squeezed me, he'd get blood before he got money. He turned on the charm and said that he didn't need money, his lady friend was generous. He insisted he just wanted to touch base, after all I was his only child. I didn't tell him that I knew he was lying. Mom had told me about at least one other child. We left one another smiling on the outside but I was madder 'n' hell on the inside. I couldn't guess what he was feeling."

I had not learned much about Adrian Cash but I had the opening I needed to ask about Betty Cash.

❧ 11 ❧

To keep the conversation going I asked, "Can I get you more coffee? I see they have sandwiches and fruit, maybe…?"

"I'll have one of those bananas, and another latte. I'll pay for this round."

But I insisted on treating and carried the fruit and our cups of latte back to the low table in front of our chairs. Fortunately the hour was a slack time and no one was hovering to take our seats. I took up my notebook and pen again and asked,

"I've heard of a woman named Betty Cash. Is she related to you?"

Glenda froze into a statue, the cup of latte in her hand quivered. Her face was grim, her eyes were bleak, her lips were pressed tightly together. When she spoke, her words came out slowly and cautiously chosen.

"Betty is Adrian's illegitimate daughter by a stripper whose stage name is Dolly Hack. Cash is a name she took; she's got no legal right to it. I have avoided any relationship with her."

"I've been trying to get in touch with her for information on Adrian. Word had it she and he were pretty tight in his last days. But she's gone missing. No one I've talked to has any idea where she might be. I thought perhaps you…."

Glenda's reaction was vehement. "No! No! I don't know and don't want to know. She's a dyed-in-the-wool bitch. If she was hanging around Adrian, it was to get money or favors out of him. Her and that boyfriend of hers might even have offed Adrian, although I never saw anything in the papers to justify an accusation. It was just that I wouldn't put homicide past the two of them if there was any advantage to be gained."

Glenda was red-faced with anger and dismay. She was swallowing her now-cool latte in big voracious gulps, but suddenly she seemed to decide to rein in her upset and assume a mask of indifference. She was so successful that I concluded she had been a pretty good actress in her day. Her performance was Oscar-worthy.

As a source of information, Glenda had gone dry. After a few trivialities and a cool farewell we parted and I started back to the Museum. I couldn't say our interview had been very useful but I had learned of Betty's boyfriend. John Wicker's report had included the name and address of the coat room attendant in Betty's defunct restaurant. I planned to try her for word of the boyfriend.

When I found Rita Keener at her apartment, she got out her little black book and read me the name, phone number and address of the boyfriend, Al Grover, on Corvina Boulevard. He apparently didn't answer his telephone; after I had left five messages on his machine, I gave up on telephoning and drove to his house. Grover lived in a gated (gated but gate unmanned) community on the beach, behind locked iron gates and locked and shuttered doors and windows. The house appeared to be three stories high and two rooms wide, walled in between other narrow beach houses, and running all the way back from the street to the beach. The courtyard in the front featured a drive leading from a wrought iron gate to a garage door and a house door. To one side was an area so sandy and studded with big boulders that it might have been a Zen garden had it been better kept. Neighbors on either side denied seeing any coming or going at the house but the woman on the south was shifty-eyed and dry-mouthed in her denial. I was sure enough of the quality of this lead that I rented a small van and bought a baseball cap. I parked the van on the opposite side of the street, donned the cap, and settled down to wait and watch. I laughed to myself. Here I was, a mild-mannered art museum employee on a stakeout. I had never had to go to these lengths on any other of the art location jobs I had pulled off. Oh well, charge it up to new experiences. I hoped the baseball cap was enough of a disguise to ward off suspicion.

I soon learned I had something to learn about stakeouts. Nothing much happened on the daytime streets of a beachfront community, booooring! Next time I would bring along a good dull book I'd been meaning to reread anyway. Furthermore, wisdom commanded provision for food, drink, and access to sanitary facilities. These latter considerations, and the fact that twilight was turning into darkness, sent me back to my office to write up my notes. A burger at the Student Commons and a quick shuffle through the mail finished off the day. In the mail was one of Agnes Emmons elegant notes commanding my presence as soon as possible to report progress. I pretended I hadn't read it; I didn't have that much to share with Agnes, and even less that I wanted to let her in on. I went home to my lodging, then like Pepys "and so to bed."

The next day at 7 A.M., armed with *War and Peace*, two bottles of water, three snack packages of cheese and crackers, and well-informed as to a filling station within walking distance, I took up my position again. No action by 11:45 when I made a quick trip to the filling station. Just as I returned, Grover's iron gate swung open, the garage door went up, and a smart black Jaguar backed out to the street. My notebook and pencil were inside the van, but I had enough time to memorize the license number and catch a glimpse of a long-haired driver, male or female I couldn't tell. By the time I got the van unlocked and started, the Jag was out of sight. I prowled around the neighborhood for a few minutes to see if I could catch up with it but had no luck. I decided to go back to the Museum and see if Jonesy had a contact at the BMV to verify the owner of the license number, Al Grover or Betty Cash. Maybe that was a long shot but Jonesy had a whole spectrum of unexpected connections; it was worth trying.

Jonesy said he would have to think and even if he made a connection, it was bound to take time. He asked me if I knew what Betty Cash looked like. Of course, I didn't but it seemed reasonable to find out. The next few days I spent on stakeout on Corvina Boulevard. The evenings I spent at the microfiche machines of the two local newspapers, hoping for a feature on the opening (or closing) of Betty's restaurant. I finally found quite a long article about The Victory, Betty's optimistic choice of name for her venture. From a grainy photo I could infer she was fair, fat, and forty. I printed the article and clipped the photo; maybe Mr. Magella could clean it up to get a better image. When consulted, Mrs. Magella said she could do better than that; she sent me to the paper's photographer who gave me a print of the original. I could see then that Betty was rather good-looking, not fat although definitely full-figured, her face sculpted in a feminine form of Adrian's bone structure, an attractive smiling expression, thick, softly waving blonde hair. No one resembling the photo came or went from the beach house; in fact, no one at all came or went. After five days, I gave up, motivated by disappointment and too much attention from local residents.

I came back to the office one afternoon to find Agnes Emmons pacing the hall, her brow like thunder, her heels hammering the marble tiles. When I saw her, I thought now there's the definition of high dudgeon. She saw me and exploded,

"Why haven't you responded to my note? Where have you been? I'm not paying you to avoid me. I want to know what you have accomplished, if anything."

I invited her into my office, pushed a pile of books off the one visitor's chair, and invited her to sit down. I was icy cool but polite. She found that disarming. She slammed her exquisitely clad bottom into the chair and ripped off her stylish kid gloves, making an effort to swallow her wrath. Her next words were less heated.

"I thought you would keep me informed of your progress. I've been so worried, fearing you were as luckless as the detectives. Please tell me you have had some success."

I told her I had followed up on all the persons who had had any connection with Cash and the Object. And that, now I was trying to find Betty Cash by tracking a person known to be her boyfriend.

"If the boyfriend is supposed to be Al Grover, he was never her boyfriend and I doubt you'll find him. Al put up most of the money for the restaurant and although he probably bedded Betty for the hell of it from time to time—she's 46 if she's a day, and he's 24—he wasn't about to play more than one-night stands. The reason he's not out and about is that he ran off to Mexico when the restaurant folded. He was laundering mob money and the Feds got on to him."

"Mrs. Emmons, how do you know all this?" I said in surprise.

She blushed slightly before replying. "He made a play for me a few days after I met him at The Victory. He was so charming and so ingratiating, I was tempted. But I have learned a little something in my 58 years; I had him investigated and didn't take the bait."

Shaving 20 years off her age in this conversation was evidence she had indeed been tempted.

"Have you a written report you can give me? He is the *only* lead I have to Betty Cash and the way things have shaken out, she's the *only* person I can connect to the picture within recent memory. Whether or not I find *him*, what I find out about him might give me a line on Betty. Incidentally, who do you think might use or live in his house on Corvina Boulevard?"

"I can give you the investigator's report; I'll send it over tomorrow with my chauffeur. Whoever is in his house, I can't say. I do know he is still in Mexico. A friend of mine ran into him in Cancun, looking seedy and cadging drinks from tourists. By the way, how is your advance money holding out?"

"You're kind to inquire but I'm managing it very well. I didn't know you expected me to turn in an expense sheet."

She snorted in amusement, "Hardly. I was just curious. I still haven't decided whether you are a smart aleck or a smart cookie. Will you let me know when—notice I say when, not if—you find Betty?"

"Maybe," I answered. I was making no promises. Who knows what Mrs. Agnes Power-Player Emmons would try if she knew too much? I didn't want her mixed up in my search. I was already regretting what

I had told her so far. She decided not to take notice of my answer. She smoothed on her gloves, settled the collar of her smart suit, and left, dismissing *my* existence in *my* office with a condescending wave. What a woman, I thought, what a woman. If I knew her better, I would probably detest her. As matters stood, I simply found her interesting.

❧ 12 ❦

As I sat thinking about Agnes, my mind wandered back to my interview with Glenda Carter and I recalled she had told me the name of Betty Cash's mother. A rummage of the phone books within reach was unproductive so I got on the Internet and Googled Dolly Hack. I found her Web site; she offered lessons in exotic dancing. Her repertoire included ecdysiastic, ballroom, and belly dancing as well as Spanish classics such as rumba, salsa, samba, and tango. She listed snail-mail and e-mail addresses, wire and cell phone numbers, emphasizing voice mail on both. Clearly she wanted to give a potential client every means of access to her services. Half a dozen photos of various terpsichorean flourishes were attached to whet a casual interest.

The next morning, before Agnes's chauffeur arrived with the report on Al Grover, I drove over to Dolly Hack's studio. The neighborhood was pretty seedy and the paint on the sign over the studio door was peeling. A placard on the door said OPEN at 11:00 and since it was only 10:30, I dropped in at the next door "bookstore" and immediately regretted my impulse. The "books" were soft porn, some masquerading as scholarly dissertations of the temple carvings of Angkor Wat and similar monuments, some as adventure comics with remarkably endowed heroes and heroines. Among the other offerings were videotapes and DVD's with suggestive titles, which suggestions I was reluctant to understand. Over a door on the back wall hung a sign "ESOTERICA," and while I was looking for the way out of ranks of book stacks that reached to the ceiling, the proprietor cornered me to ask if I would like the key to the ESOTERICA. I refused politely and hastened to leave, hoping no one had seen me go in or come out. I went down to the corner filling station and asked for the key to the rest room where I washed my hands. Twice! I emerged and saw with relief that my watch read 10:55. A small woman in a full-body black leotard and high-heeled black boots was unlocking Dolly Hack's door and as I approached, she smiled and waved me inside. Retreating behind a counter in the foyer, the woman smiled even more brightly as she asked,

"And what can I do for you, dearie? We have a special on this week. Ten lessons for a hundred dollars, regularly one fifty."

"I was hoping to speak to Ms. Hack. Is she in?" I hazarded.

"Miz Hack, that's me. Call me Dolly. I don't stand on ceremony with my patrons."

Dolly was what I had seen described as a "pocket Venus," a little shorter than my 5 foot 4, generously endowed as to bosom and hips, tiny waist, Rubenesque on a small scale. Her hair was professionally dyed and done, a soft golden brown in all-over curls. Bright brown eyes sparkled in a carefully made up face, the age wrinkles barely obvious. The eyes grew shrewd under slightly lowered lids when I asked,

"I've been trying to get in touch with Betty Cash. I was told you were related to her and I thought perhaps you might know her current address."

"What for?"

I started into my handy lie about an Adrian Cash book but before I had got well into my spiel, Dolly interrupted.

"You want to know something about Adrian Cash, you talk to me. I can tell you what the movie magazines and tabloids never published, namely the truth! I been lookin' for somebody to sell, er, tell my story to."

She cocked her head to one side and favored me with a wink. Just then, the shop door banged open to admit a lanky young man with clothes in a cleaner's bag over his shoulder.

"Yer late!" Dolly snapped. "Hurry and get changed, Mrs. Beeman's due in 10 minutes and she's one of our best customers."

The young man ducked his head and disappeared into the back room. Dolly beckoned me into a small untidy room which she called her office, leaving the door open. She had made up her mind about something.

"You want information about Adrian Cash. How much is it worth to you?" she asked.

"I'd think you were the one to say how much it's worth to you." I replied.

"Five hundred?"

"I won't haggle. Five hundred it is."

I could see she was already regretting an answer too promptly given. I could almost see the numbers turning over in her head. But I had the money and I was going to gamble that this investment would get me to Betty Cash.

"But how do I know whether I'd get value for the money? I don't have that kind of money on me. I'll write a check...."

"You'll get value," Dolly said firmly. She wasn't about to let this fish get away. "Cash," she said. "Or no deal. There's an ATM in the grocery store over on the next street. I'll wait."

The deal was done. When I returned an hour later with ten crisp 50s, the lanky dancer in shiny skin-tight black pants and a white silk shirt with billowing sleeves and the neck open almost to his navel was escorting Mrs. Beeman out. Mrs. Beeman was a respectable middle-aged middle-class matron who departed sedately in a late model Buick, apparently elated by a successful dancing lesson. Dolly was waiting, and I forked over the bills and took out my pad and pencil. She told me her sad little story, a snatch-and-grab liaison with Adrian Cash which got her out of the strip club but left her with a baby, cashless (she snickered at her feeble joke) and on welfare. A reprise of Glenda's story, just a little more tawdry. She went on to say her luck had turned when she met her current husband, a musician in an modestly successful rock band, and after they had scraped together enough to open her dance studio, she was doing fairly well. She hadn't kept in touch with Adrian in his later years; he always wanted money and she had told him to get lost with a gun in her hand. He had taken the hint. She added little to my picture of Adrian Cash but the mention of a baby opened the door to a question about Betty.

"Somebody told me Betty Cash is your daughter and that she had buddied up to Adrian a while before he died. I've been trying to locate her. The last chapter of the book depends on what she can tell me about Adrian."

"Yeah," Dolly drawled. "She's hiding out. That restaurant was a bad idea, the sort of flop that keeps on flopping. She's still got creditors after her. I don't see her but I get a phone call every week or so, asking for grocery money. I send her a money order. We aren't close, don't even like one another much, but whatcha gonna do? You can't let your own kid go hungry, now can you?" Her face softened for a moment then went grim, then expressionless.

"Do you have an address for her? If five hundred is coming in handy for you, maybe she would…."

"She sure would, but I have to check with her first." Dolly started punching numbers on her phone; with her other hand she shielded them from me. She spoke briefly then listened. When she turned to me, she said,

"Betty says if you are buying information, she'll sell. But don't come around until Monday, she expects to be gone over the weekend. Write down 15335 West Ridge Canyon Drive in Altamor. She'll be home all day."

I left then, resolving to arm myself with a generous wad of cash before Monday. I noticed a battered Dodge Dart pulling away from the curb as I drove away. It followed me for a few blocks until I was well on my way back to the Museum, then dropped from sight.

❧ 13 ❧

Back at the museum I found a note from Jonesy stuck on my door and Agnes's report on Al Grover on my desk. Jonesy's note read:

"Don't forget the wine and cheese thing for the Theta Pi alumnae this evening, seven to ten in the Egyptian wing. *Dress up!*"

I had forgotten, but if I left the Grover report till tomorrow morning and rushed over to the Commons to gobble something for dinner, I would have time to go home and do myself up for the affair. I took an unscheduled shower (Zulu wasn't home to scold) and dressed in my reception uniform, a black sheath with one bare shoulder, panty hose, and heels. My gamine haircut was holding up pretty well and I had to admit my glittery dime-store dangling earrings showed to good advantage. A splash of bright red lipstick and a squirt of Opium (cologne) and I was ready for an evening of mingling on behalf of the Museum's financial well-being. The Theta Pis were generous patrons but boring conversationalists. But they did drag along some interesting husbands from time to time.

I was mingling more or less graciously with a glass of white wine in my hand when I found myself standing beside a rather handsome fellow who appeared to fall into my age category. He smiled and raised his glass to me,

"This is a quite a nice do, isn't it?"

I agreed and made some literate comments on a nearby stele of Ramses II while I gave the man a once-over. Stocky, a couple of inches taller than me in my 2-inch heels—a point I always checked when a promising male hove into view—thick curls of auburn hair, sharp and acutely intelligent grey eyes, left hand ring finger bare. Wine and a relaxed social occasion was making me a great deal more observant of the opposite sex than I was as a rule. His next words woke me from my brief daydream.

"It seems we have a mutual acquaintance in Dolly Mead, Hack, that is. I saw you leaving her shop earlier today."

"Oh, yes," I trotted out my handy somewhat shopworn lie. "I'm working on a book about movie personalities and she knew Adrian Cash in the old days."

"Surprising choice of subject for a museum curator of antiquities. But people have unexpected hobbies, don't they? Myself, I was a grad student with Dr. Jones, did my thesis on ancient musical instruments, and now I do tax audits for the government. That's a right angle turn on a classical education, don't you agree?".

"I did my thesis with Dr. Jones, too. It explored changes in styles of ushebtis between the early and late dynasties." At his puzzled look, I explained, "Those little figurines the old Egyptians tucked into the mummy's wrappings, images of people to do the work expected of the dead in the hereafter. There's a whole case full of them over there by that lady who's signaling to you. Is she your wife?"

Neat segue, I thought.

"No, my sister. Her husband was tied up this evening and she wanted an escort. Since I am unattached, I often fill in for Harry. Keeps Sally happy and wins me many a good Sunday dinner by way of reward. Did you bring a husband?"

That was direct. I decided to be equally direct. "No, I'm not married, are you?"

"Nope. That's why I'd like to invite you to dinner and a movie Saturday evening. Are you free?"

Just then, Jonesy bustled up to us.

"Ah," he said, "two of my favorite students in the same place at the same time. Did anybody introduce you? No? Then I will! Zima Crenshaw meet Benjamin Conrad. Ben meet Zima. How about another glass of wine for each of you? Celebration! The Theta Pi Foundation has just given us $200,000. Reason enough for me to sound like a blithering idiot."

And he hustled off to greet the Dean of the School of Fine Arts with the good news. Ben and I stood looking at one another in silent amazement. Then we laughed, and Ben said,

"Where were we? If I remember correctly, Ms. Zima, I was trying to make a date with you. What do you say?"

"I say, yes, thank you for asking. Tell me where and when."

And we laughed some more. Ben's sister came over then to whisk him away, pleading a call from the sitter. Before they left, he introduced us. Her name was Sally Kretzman and she and her husband ran a computer company. Soon after, the hall emptied and I got to go home. It was fortunate indeed that home was within walking distance. I've never been sure whether it was too much wine or head in the clouds as I dwelt on a date with Ben, but my feet seemed not to touch the ground all the way.

The next morning I arrived at the office rather bleary-eyed but heartened by a breakfast of strong black coffee and sugary oatmeal at the Commons. Of course, the first thing I saw on my desk was Al Grover's dossier. It was quite a packet. To give Agnes credit, when she gave orders to investigate, she meant it and the investigator complied. One of the first things I learned was that the black Jag that had left Al Grover's Corvina Boulevard house was more or less Al Grover's. The plate number I had taken down was in his name, but the payments had been in arrears for months. Only a charitable dealer or a beneficent friend had staved off the "Repo Man" that I suspected had driven it away. I wondered what else he had repossessed from inside the house.

Grover was a handsome lad, college dropout, career layabout, who lived off wealthy women taken in by his charms. He often had two or three on the string at a time. Where he got the money to partner with Betty Cash in the restaurant was something of a mystery but the investigator had listed several of Al's cronies who had friends with dubious connections. The investigator believed that tracing the tortuous connections would lead to mob figures but it would take time and money. Agnes was unwilling to go to that extent and called him off. Al Grover wasn't exactly a dead end but he wasn't a very lively lead. I filed the report away; I could always go back to it if indications warranted. My best bet was confrontation with Betty Cash on Monday.

In the meantime, I set myself to daydreaming and planning my wardrobe for Saturday's fling. To fuel my daydreams I spent some time looking up Ben Conrad's academic background and pumping Jonesy.

"Ben Conrad. Well, when I said he was a favorite student, I told no lie. Smart as a whip, a hard worker, did excellent research, had a real flair for novel insights. If I recall, his thesis was a joy to read. I never really understood his decision to go for an M.F.A., his undergrad degree was in business with a minor in ancient languages. When I pushed him to try for a Ph.D., even got him a grant, he said no thanks, he was going to work for some government agency, as an accountant for God's sakes! I finally gave up on him, decided he was one of those kids who can't commit to a single career until he's tried a variety. He was only 20 when I handed him his Master's degree."

"And that makes him what? now?"

"Mmmm, 32, 33 I think. Why are you asking?"

I admitted to accepting an invitation to go out with him. Jonesy approved.

"You work too hard. When was the last time you went out with a nice fella your own age?"

"When was it you took me to see *Ishtar* at the Cinema Center?"

The conversation ended in laughter and a highly critical review of the worst movie of the century. I returned to planning my wardrobe. I even went so far as to go shopping for a new dress, nothing fancy I told myself, nothing expensive. So much for good intentions. I ended up with a silky, dull gold gown with a cowl neckline, and bought black enamel costume jewelry to go with it, namely a pin to highlight the cowl and dangling earrings because I felt sexy when I tried them on. Zulu approved of my choices and loaned me her African paisley print stole to finish me off.

I had a wonderful time on my date. I don't even remember what we ate at dinner. Ben and I seemed to have an unlimited supply of topics to talk about. He was so witty that I was inspired to get off a few *bon mots* myself. I hadn't had so much fun in a long time, and I told him so.

"Me, too," he replied. "What do you say to a repeat performance next Saturday?. I have to go out of town on a job tomorrow and probably won't get back till Friday. How about I call you when I get in to settle the details?"

Of course, I said. We said good by at the Puckett door, and I went up the stairs to my light blue room with my heart singing. I could barely remember what Giovane looked like, and didn't care.

∞ 14 ∞

The next morning I rose clear-headed and went to the Commons for a pancake breakfast and the Sunday papers. I strolled back to Puckett House planning to loll away a lazy day. But entering the house, I saw Mrs. Puckett sprawled on the floor at the foot of the stairs in the back hall. She had fallen and hadn't been able to make herself heard. In the subsequent flurry, my plans for a lazy day quickly evaporated. I called 9-1-1 and Mrs. Puckett's son; he was on the golf course and said he would meet us at the ER. Then to quell Mrs. Puckett's frantic fears, I hunted up her purse

"It's got all my medical papers in it and this week's rent money," she wailed.

I accompanied her to the ER in the ambulance and tended her belongings while they carted her around for mysterious scans and tests. I was greatly relieved when Amos Puckett turned up in Bermuda shorts and an Argyle sweater and seemingly as cool as a cucumber. When the doctors told him his mother had suffered a broken hip and pelvis and would require complicated surgery and a long convalescence, his self-possession melted into tears. He was a large beefy man, a prominent attorney accustomed to taking charge, but now he put his head in his hands and cried. I stood by him, patting his shoulder, hoping he would get hold of himself so I could turn over Mrs. Puckett's purse and leave. He regained his equanimity at last, thanked me for my attention to "Mama," and promised to come around to the house later in the day. It was about nine in the evening when he came, assuring the tenants that Mama was resting quietly and that he would arrange for someone to look after the house. The someone was Zulu, who was to be assisted by a junior from his office. Her rent was to be forgiven while she did the job. She was torn between sorry for Mrs. Puckett and elated over the financial windfall.

The next morning I packed up pen and pad in my purse and headed for Altamor. West Ridge Canyon Drive was a street of nondescript houses hastily built in the 50s to house WW II veterans. Most were in a state of incipient terminal decay; 15335 was no exception. Its screened-in front porch displayed flaps of screening drooping in rags from the door frame and windows. I pushed aside the porch door carefully lest it fall off in my hand and approached the house door which stood wide open. Yoohooing, I knocked and when there was no answer, entered still calling out. The interior of the house was decrepit but not particularly dirty. A living room furnished with a cheap, rickety, upholstered "suite" occupied the full width of the house. A hall led to the back rooms, on the right a kitchen with a breakfast nook, on the left two minuscule bedrooms, one of them with an open door. I called out again as I put my head through the door but fell silent when I spotted a woman, surely Betty Cash, sprawled prone on the floor. She wore a housecoat rucked up over her hips and one fuzzy house slipper. Yogi's catch phrase *déjà vu* all over again flitted through my mind. Mrs. Puckett's fall fresh in my memory, I went to Betty and reached for her wrist. It was cold,

cold, cold and pulseless. She was dead. I stood over her shocked and stunned by the realization.

When my brain functioned again, I noted that her face lay buried in a bed pillow smeared with dried blood. Gingerly I lifted her head slightly, disclosing her nose and badly bruised lips as sources of the blood. Her condition was not due to a fall, it was homicide either accidental or intentional. I remembered a TV program in which the detectives had identified a bed pillow crushed over the face of the victim as the fatal means to cause death by suffocation. I backed away, not daring to investigate the body further. On my right there was a disheveled bed, on the left a bureau with all the drawers pulled out. Then I spotted it: scraps of red, white, and blue wood, the frame of the Object. It was lying half-concealed by the tumble of sheets on the bed. The frame was empty; scraps of photo paper fringed the inside edge. With my pencil I tipped it over to reveal the back side. Pry marks showed where the wooden slats of the painting had been pried free; a few threads of gessoed canvas still clung to one of the marks.

What to do? Betty Cash dead, murdered, the Rembrandt gone who knew where. I dreaded the potential fallout of explanations police would require. Questions like why had I come to Betty's house and worse, what was the reason for a damaged picture frame. Newspaper attention, word of a missing two million dollar painting leaking out, ideas whirling in my mind coalesced into a single urgent mandate: GET OUT OF HERE! I found some unused Kleenex in my purse and polished every spot I might have touched on my way to Betty's bedroom. Although I had seen a telephone in the living room and I had my cell phone in my purse, I remembered that police could trace any call made by either means. I would have to find a pay phone somewhere distant from West Ridge Canyon Drive. I looked up and down and across the street before I stepped off the porch and scurried for my car. I hoped I had come and was leaving unobserved.

I had to make two passes down Altamor's main street before I found a working pay phone on the side of a cut-rate grocery store. A partially defaced sticker provided an emergency number. I punched the buttons with the eraser of my pencil, cursing myself for a caution that was probably uncalled for. To the crisp female voice that said,

"Altamor Police Department, how may I direct your call?"

I babbled, "There's a dead woman, murdered I think, at 15335 West Ridge Canyon Drive. She's been dead for a while already." And hung up before any questions could be asked.

I hurried into my car and drove to the Museum, fighting tears and nausea at the same time. My hands shook so badly I had trouble fitting my card into the slot at the gate of the parking lot. I sat breathing deeply for a good five minutes before getting out and going into the building. I headed for Jonesy's office; his secretary was probably out to lunch, at least the outer office was empty. I burst into the inner office without knocking and flipped the lock on the door knob behind me. Jonesy was sitting at his computer, a half-eaten cheese sandwich and an apple on the desk blotter. He looked up startled at my boisterous entrance.

"What's wrong? My God, you look like the world is coming to an end! What's happened?"

"Oh, Jonesy, I found Betty Cash and she's dead, murdered I think, and the Rembrandt has been torn out of the frame and God knows where it is. What shall I do?"

"Well, the first thing to do is sit down and begin your story at the beginning and for God's sake, don't cry!"

As always, he had got right to the heart of the matter. I took a minute or so to get control of my breathing, then I told him the whole story of my morning. He listened attentively, head tilted to one side, nibbling at the apple from time to time. When I finished and subsided into silence, he laid aside his apple core and began with the questions.

"Are you sure she was dead? Are you sure it was the Rembrandt that was ripped out of the frame?"

"Oh, yes," I assured him. "She was dead. And what else could have left threads of 17th century canvas in the ravaged fame?" I suddenly felt empty, like a glass that had just been drained of its contents. Jonesy's voice buzzed and echoed in the emptiness of my head. I hadn't fainted but I had certainly left the real world. Jonesy's hand shaking my shoulder brought me back into it.

"Are you OK? Shall I get one of the girls to help you to the couch in the women's room?"

I refused that and asked, "What have I done wrong? What shall I do now? Should I talk to the police, tell them all of what I know, part of it, any of it? What?"

Jonesy's face was very serious as he replied, "I don't know. Maybe you should just sit tight. I got to admit you have yourself between a rock and a hard place. If you can keep your cool and keep your mouth shut while you wait it out, maybe the next events will shake themselves out and get you off the hook. I'm the only one who's heard this story and my lips are sealed."

I considered his words, then asked, "Do you mind if I take a few days off? Maybe if I distract myself with a few days of vacation, I'll be able to see my way more clearly."

With Jonesy's blessing, that's what I did.

❧ 15 ✍

I headed into the mountains. Just driving the pine-scented roads was soothing. Arriving at the Franciscan Retreat House, I parked and sat in the car for 10 minutes with the windows open, looking around and breathing deeply of the fresh mountain air. Vast scarps and white-capped peaks loomed over the green valleys of the rolling foothills where the rustic lodge nestled almost out of sight in a flowery hollow. Only bird song and the soft whisper of a warm breeze invaded the peace and isolation of the scene. A hawk soared on the updrafts of the sun-warmed skies. Gratefully I noted there were only two other cars in the lot. Good, that meant a sparse attendance at meals and freedom from unwanted conversation. I had come in the past to the Retreat House when living in the Crenshaw house had become unbearable, for weekends usually. The place was often more patronized on weekends than I wanted but the house rule "Speak only if spoken to" kept the peace when larger numbers of guests were staying.

I hauled my bag out of the car and started down a graveled path to the lodge. Built of rough-hewn logs with a sprawling veranda, it was the hub of several radiating paths that led over and around the hills to quiet vistas and occasionally to small watercourses. World weariness fading, I planned with reborn enthusiasm to hunt up the beaver pond. Sitting on a bench there one could watch adult beavers teaching their kits how to grow up Beaver. Their antics were amusing and their quiet persistence as they went about their chores was inspiring. Visiting the beaver pond was like going to a part of town where I used to live to see what had been built or torn down since I was there last. In contrast to urban development, however, change at the beaver pond was part of the cosmic plan. It was reassuring, not threatening. I had put hiking boots in my bag counting on undemanding climbs over a favorite rocky hill. I never did that climb without coming back with scratches and bruises on my hands. That, too, was part of the cosmic plan. The hurt was a reminder that men had conquered this landscape on foot, not by wheels rolling over tarmac and concrete paving. Reaching the top and flopping on a warm boulder was more than an achievement, it was an experience. I could think long, important thoughts up there, thoughts that were well-nigh impossible anywhere else. Pure thoughts, impure thoughts, good thoughts, evil thoughts, God was so close His presence accepted and forgave all.

Brother St. John popped out of a back room as the front door closed behind me. With a welcoming smile, he pushed the visitor's book toward me over the counter and took down a key from a hook on the wall behind him. Neither of us spoke, smiles and nods served as communication. Silence was not mandated, it was simply comfortable and customary. The tag on the key directed me to my favorite room, a cell on the southeast corner of the second floor, furnished with a simple table and chair, a single bed with a gray wool blanket, and a set of shelves on which to place one's books or one's underwear. I knew that the bathroom was down the hall, very plain fixtures but a window that framed a magnificent view of the most splendid alp of the range filling the horizon. My mood had lightened so much that I chuckled when I found a white-footed field mouse scurrying around behind the toilet. St. Francis would have picked him up for a caress. Not me, I just waved my good wishes at him and went about my business. The card on the back of the room door carried the familiar message: "Breakfast 6-7, lunch 12-1, dinner 6-7, refrigerator raids unscheduled." I changed into outdoor clothes, checked my watch, and went to lunch.

Five people in the dining room, not counting the other Brother John, the one affectionately known as Brother Demi-John for his very short stature. He waved me to my choice of seats and brought utensils, napkin, and water glass, then went to the kitchen from which he returned juggling a plate of spaghetti and meatballs, garlic bread on the side, a bowl of salad greens, and a pitcher of milk. Condiments and a bowl of apples and oranges on the table completed the fare. He lingered briefly at my side, head bowed, hands folded, lips moving in a silent grace to bless my meal. As always, the food was delicious.

The beaver visit occupied my afternoon. The current crop of kits was half-grown and already beginning to gnaw on the alders in the thicket on the opposite side of the pond. A granddaddy beaver crouched on the highest part of the dam, grooming himself with a claw on his back foot, the claw the Creator had given him for just that purpose. Since I had been here last someone had built a backrest on the bench; in my unexpected comfort, I relaxed and fell into a doze. I woke to a SPLAT! Granddaddy's big flat tail hitting the water in a warning. Kits made mini-fountains splashing into the water. The coyote prowling lazily on the far side of the pond looked up briefly and went on his way. I followed his example and wandered just as lazily through a stand of aspens where a deer herd congregated in the winter. None of the deer were home this day although there was plenty of evidence of a well-populated yard. I waded through a nearby rivulet to clean my boots before starting back to the lodge.

One went to bed early at the Retreat House; there wasn't much else to do. There were no clocks at the House, although peals of bells at 6, 9, noon, 3, 6, 9, midnight and again at 3 counted off the hours of the day. Familiars of the House heard them without especially noticing. I lay quietly under my wool blanket, gazing out the uncurtained windows at stars burning in the deep blue sky. Over and over in my mind, I revolved my quandary.

I knew I was obliged to talk to the police and to be truthful. The quandary was how much and what to tell them. Betty Cash deserved every break that would lead to her killer, but Agnes also deserved to get her Rembrandt back. Would talking to the police help find a killer but talking about the painting jeopardize its recovery? I had to admit that so far my effort to recover Giovane was a big fat bust. Would involving the police improve my prospects? Whoever had killed Betty undoubtedly now had Giovane. Catching the killer might find the Rembrandt. Finding the Rembrandt might catch the killer. But my thinking stopped there because I fell asleep.

The next day I climbed my rocky hill and perched on the topmost boulder. Although sunshine prevailed, a few clouds sailing across the sky cast momentary shadows, and the breeze was sharp. After a few minutes I sought shelter in a cranny farther down. I could still enjoy a glorious view of the mountains and the sky but without freezing my ears off. In the pleasant warmth of the nook, my thoughts returned to Giovane. In my memory his sidelong gaze seemed more malicious than teasing. Or was it Adrian's photo, overlaid on Giovane's portrait, that conveyed malice more than humor? After all, Adrian's mimicking Giovane's pose had no kind intent. Adrian had bested Agnes's memory of her Adonis, he intended his photo to display triumph. I knew how cruel human relations could be, I was a victim. My family's unconscious cruelty had no active expression; the cruelty was simple indifference to my need to be loved, to be valued. Now I was seeing Adrian's conscious cruelty. Agnes had to be humiliated and his photo overlying a valuable symbol of a young and virile lover was a subtle but severe insult. I wondered if she had realized that. Perhaps she was too engrossed in herself to know that Adrian had probably despised, even hated, her and his dependence on her. I was suddenly aware that I was indulging in bargain basement psychology for which I had no qualifications, uselessly mulling mere second-rate speculation.

In the far distance I heard the peal of the House bell. Noon. I shook myself out of my daydreams and opened the brown bag in which I had assembled an *al fresco* lunch. Ham sandwich, an apple, two Oreos, and a bottle of Evian—I ate and drank with relish, diverted by the antics of a ground squirrel. He was fearless, bouncing around on a rock not three feet from me, flirting his tail saucily, and cheerfully exclaiming "Chirk! Chirk!" I rewarded the entertainment with bits of crust from my sandwich. He stuffed his cheeks full then disappeared to return moments later with uncles, aunts, sisters, brothers, cousins—in a word, his whole family. When I ran out of crust, I handed out apple core. When that had been demolished, the whole bunch of them vanished. "Outta crumbs, outta consideration," I remarked philosophically to the empty landscape. My silly saying reminded me that I still hadn't decided which crumbs of my recent findings I would feed the police. Nor how much consideration I might expect if I chose to give them the whole crust. Dope, I told myself, you've got to quit turning every notion into a paradigm of your predicament!

I climbed down from the hill and took the tree-lined path to a waterfall that an enthusiastic guest had labeled "the bridal veil." I could admit the justice of the name; a scanty flow of water over a rocky lip broke into gauzy mist as it hit the granite shelves of the cliff. Below and on either side of the fall, which was at most 20 or 25 feet high and only five or six feet wide, lush and leafy growth hedged the shallow creek. The music of the water was only a whisper of sound. I sat down on a rock and shed shoes and socks to soak my feet, aching from the climb up and down the hill. The water was icy cold and I cut my soak short. While I sat there, a fox came to drink. She looked at me incuriously and unalarmed as she bent to drink. I mused that the mouse population must be numerous this year, her plump body and shiny pelt spoke to good health and ample nutrition. I dawdled the afternoon away on paths that I knew well and ended up at the House in time to shower and change into clean shirt and jeans for dinner. A card propped against the catsup bottle on my table announced a concert of classical music, CDs to be played in the lounge at 7:30. In the lounge, another card propped against the CD player announced it was the gift of "A Friend of the House." A beaming Brother Demi-John placed a stack of CDs next to the player and loaded the first on it. This was a new departure for the House, kindly meant and kindly received. I went to bed snippets of *Ode to Joy* and *Fingal's Cave* running through my mind. I fell asleep the moment my head hit the pillow. No introspection tonight.

I had planned to go walking on Wednesday morning, but at breakfast Brother St. John advised us that a female bear and her cubs were hanging around the woods. The bear was a frequent visitor, hoping unsuccessfully for unsecured leavings of fruit and vegetables. The brothers, however, maintained their compost pile in a locked shed and took great pains to lead her not into temptation. I chose to stay in and make frequent use of the binoculars hanging next to the front window of the lounge. A small library of dog-eared paperback books and magazines left behind by previous guests provided an eclectic selection of reading materials. The spectrum of authors included Kierkegaard, Spillane, Melville, and William S. Shirer. The National Geographics were vintage, some as old as 1976, some as new as last month. There was even a devotional booklet for a Ba-ha'i service. My trips to the window to view the scenery were rewarded finally by Mama Bear's advent, trailed by her two unruly cubs. She made a leisurely ambit around the House, sniffing hopefully at this or that promising source of a snack, then lying down for a nap in a patch of yellow Coreopsis. After a milky snack, the cubs escaped her motherly control long enough to gambol across the veranda and turn over two small pots of geraniums. She called them away with peremptory grunts and the three of them wandered off in the direction of the beaver pond. It was close to four o'clock and I still had the National Geographic issue detailing the explosion of Mount St. Helens to read, and so to dinner and so to bed. I had not given more than a minute or two all day to thinking about my quandary, but the night was devoted to it.

I rose on Thursday morning, committed to a visit to the Altamor Police on my way home from the Retreat House. I was still unsure of what I would divulge but I had rehearsed an opening sentence. I planned to put it this way:

"I was recently engaged by a wealthy woman to recover a very valuable painting which had been missing for some 12 years. She had recently had word of it in the hands of Betty Cash. I was calling on Ms. Cash to interview her when I found her dead. Too shocked to be sensible, I made an anonymous call to the station and took refuge at the Franciscan Retreat House since then, trying to regain my composure."

Maybe I would try to make it more grammatical. Then I would wait to see what transpired.

∞ 16 ∞

I took one more walk in the valley, although I had to borrow rain gear to cope with the drizzly mist that had developed during the night. The rain had not soaked the landscape, only moistened the flora and heightened the colors and fresh odors of grass and trees and wildflowers. I came in, packed my bag, left my donation on the bureau, and bade farewell to Brother St. John. He raised his hand in silent smiling blessing for safe travel on my way home. I had often wondered how the Brothers assigned to serve the Retreat House survived months at a time in the wilderness. I knew that they received a week's worth of newspapers, delivered on Saturday morning with the groceries and gas for the generator. I knew that their days and nights were busy, cooking and cleaning for the Retreat House, tending a vegetable garden in the summer, shoveling snow in the winter, doing laundry, attending chapel for prayer and meditation four times a day. But they glided around so unobtrusively in their long brown habits, faces often hidden in their cowls, I wondered if they knew or even cared what went on outside the valley. They lived Peace, a peace I envied but knew I could never achieve by the means they had chosen. I drove away reassured that their world was in good hands and hopeful that mine would be the same.

The police station in Altamor was in a quaintly art deco courthouse standing in a traditional square in the middle of town. The police department was located in the basement and even in sleepy Altamor one entered through metal detectors. A brisk young policewoman presided over a counter where an overweight policeman was filling out a wad of forms.

"Yes, ma'am, how can we help you?" she said and sounded like she meant it.

"I need to talk to whomever, er whoever, is the officer in charge of investigating the murder of Betty Cash or Hack as she may be known." I was too nervous to watch my grammar.

"Yes ma'am, Detective Sergeant Tomas Rodriguez will be glad to talk to you. Just a moment while I tell him you're here. And the name is …."

"Crenshaw, Cosima, Zima, Elaine. That's Cosima Elaine Crenshaw, Zima for short." Not only did my nerves affect my grammar, I was stuttering as well.

A trim middle-aged man wearing aviator glasses, a brush cut, and a power tie over a crisp white shirt appeared from a back room and ushered me to a seat by his desk in an otherwise empty squad room. He offered coffee which I turned down and pulled out a yellow legal pad, clicked his automatic pen into operation, and looked expectantly at me. I tried out my carefully rehearsed opening sentence, but stumbled over Betty's name.

"I don't know the name she used in Altamor but it might be Cash or Hack. Anyway she's the woman I found dead in a house on West

Ridge Canyon Drive on Monday. I called to report it but didn't have the courage to give you my name."

"I have your name now. I need your address, place of employment, and your position there."

I obliged and he wrote everything down, then instructed me,

"Tell me your story, begin at the time you drove up to house that was the scene of the crime. I'll get the background later. Please tell me as exactly as you can remember what you saw or heard or did at the house."

That was pretty easy. My memory banks were trained to accumulate and retain detail and I was accustomed to describing places and things in detail. And although this was not an exercise in evaluating art objects, I could carry it off without emotion. As I related my observations, the detective took down my words in shorthand. He saved his questions until I had finished and fallen silent. The first one surprised me although it shouldn't have.

"Did you touch anything?"

"Only the woman's wrist. It was cold, no pulse, as I said."

"How did you get in?"

"The screen door was hanging open, the house door was ajar, all but one door inside the house stood wide open. I went in calling to announce my presence and when there was no answer just kept going until I saw her in the bedroom."

"Did you know her before?"

"We had never met, but in the course of my research, I had obtained good photographs of her. Her mother, Ms. Hack or Mrs. Mead, had given me her address; and I just assumed it was Betty Hack or Cash as she called herself."

"Mrs. Elizabeth Ann Hack Broward rented the rent the house on West Ridge Canyon Drive. She was the ex-wife of Howell Broward who still lives in Altamor and is a member of the police force. Didn't her mother tell you that?"

I nodded in the negative, puzzled that he was confiding this information to me. I hoped the reason would come later, now there was another question.

"Did you find a phone in the house?"

"I saw one on a table in the living room, but I was afraid to use it, for fear it had important fingerprints on it."

"Didn't you have a cell phone? Almost everyone does these days."

I know I blushed. It was hard to admit that I was afraid my identity could be traced if I used the cell phone. I stumbled through an explanation of my behavior; I knew trying to keep my identity secret when I reported Betty's death was suspicious but then and now I was still trying to protect information about the Object.

"I'm not a suspect, am I?" It was a weak attempt to change the subject.

"No, old Mrs. Houlihan is semi-invalid and spends a lot of time at her front window. She saw you arrive and leave and the timing matches your call from the pay phone. The M.E. said Mrs. Broward had been dead since Sunday morning. Her ex-husband seems to have been the last person to see her alive. Mrs. Houlihan wasn't on duty Sunday, she was away spending the day at her daughter's house. "

My tension was growing; Detective Rodriguez hadn't alluded once to the disorder in Betty's bedroom. Was he going to overlook the picture frame? Or bypass it? How might the ex-husband figure in all this? There had never been mention of him in my investigations so far.

"Now, Ms. Crenshaw, I want you to tell me why you were hunting down Mrs. Broward. Her mother told us she had sent you to her because you wanted information about her father for a book you are writing. Why is an assistant curator at the University Museum of Fine Arts dogging people for dirt about Adrian Cash? He's been dead a long time and wasn't much of a movie star while he was alive. I'd like to hear a better reason than an exposé for your interest in Adrian Cash's movie career."

I drew a deep breath and ventured on my tale.

❧ 17 ❧

I told Rodriguez I had been retained by a very wealthy woman to recover an extremely valuable painting. No, I was not a detective, but I had something of a reputation for locating highly desirable art for acquisition by the University Museum. The painting had been loaned by this woman to a friend, Adrian Cash, about 12 years ago. Due to a combination of unfortunate circumstances—Cash's death while in possession of the painting, a disguise Cash had added by way of a joke, the owner's illness which prevented timely recovery from Cash's belongings, the insurance company's failed investigation and subsequent pay off—the painting had dropped out of sight until just recently. Cash had covered the painting, which was in a distinctive frame, with a photo portrait of himself. The complex of frame, photo, and painting had been in Betty Cash's possession and on display in her restaurant as recently as last June. The frame had been painted red, white, and blue to match the décor of the restaurant, but the painting was still in the frame behind Cash's photo. Betty Cash slash Hack slash

Broward had gone into hiding, probably to avoid creditors, when her restaurant had failed.

"It would seem logical ," I said slowly and cautiously, "to believe that the broken frame I saw in Betty Cash's bedroom, with scraps of photoprint paper still attached, was the frame in which the painting had originally resided."

Rodriguez bored in at once. His questions came rapid fire.

"Who is this rich woman who engaged your services? Why is this painting so valuable? Who besides yourself knew or suspected that Betty had it?"

I gulped and blurted out the truth,

"Mrs. Agnes Cathcart DeWitt Emmons. The painting is an authentic Rembrandt and the insurance company paid out two million dollars to settle her claim."

I decided to beg. "Please try to keep this information secret. Mrs. Emmons would be very angry if word of the painting leaked to the newspapers, and she has the means to avenge herself for the indiscretion. Not only that, but publicity would probably drive the painting deeper underground and render all further attempts to recover it useless. I have been very discreet in my interviews. Probably only Mr. Wicker, the investigator Mrs. Emmons had most recently hired, and Mrs. Emmons herself knew where and how the painting was hidden. There was even a possibility that Betty did not know that the frame she had repainted contained the painting under a photograph of her father. If she had known, I think she would have tried to hawk it. She was broke and in debt. No rumors of a hitherto unknown Rembrandt have percolated through the art world, although a leak now will rapidly turn into an unprincipled scramble to locate it, by fair means or foul. "

"Maybe foul means have already been used," Rodriguez said thoughtfully. "Your investigation may have been discreet but perhaps Mrs. Broward *did* know and *she* was indiscreet. A painting worth two million dollars creates a fairly good motive for murder."

"Do you have a suspect? Didn't you say her ex-husband was the last to see her alive?"

"We're talking to him." Then suddenly, the detective looked sharply at me and I could see he was having second thoughts. He obviously had said more than he intended and now he clammed up. He instructed me to continue to be available and I was allowed to leave.

As I drove off, I was curiously relieved. I had faced my dilemma and although it had no solution, it was behind me. What was before me was my date with Ben, a very pleasant prospect. Not so pleasant was the stack of telephone messages that had accumulated on my desk at the office: one daily from Ben, two a day from Agnes Emmons starting as early as Monday afternoon, and another two today from Amos Puckett. I tackled a reply to Amos Puckett first. His secretary regretted he was tied up in court. She couldn't tell me why talking to me was so urgent, but she would suggest he contact me at Puckett House in the late afternoon. I wanted very much to reply to Ben but his messages had no number where or how I could reach him. I would just have to wait till he tried me again. I dreaded talking to Agnes Emmons, all the more since I expected Altamor detectives would have contacted her already. I did wonder what had set her off as early as Monday. I hastily scanned the daily papers but found no more than ten lines reporting Mrs. Betty Broward's suspected homicide and Altamor P.D. pursuing the case. Had Agnes known Betty's married name? Did she do something so plebeian as reading the newspapers? I called Agnes's home and spoke to the lordly butler. Yes, Mrs. Emmons was most anxious to talk to me, he had been instructed to invite me to stop by for tea at four if I should call. Today? Yes, Madam would have returned from her exercise session by that time.

Jonesy was out somewhere so I left word that I had returned but had gone to see Agnes. Then I went home and violated the shower schedule. Dressed in fresh shirt, jeans, and moccasins, I just made the 4 P.M. appointment with Agnes. She frowned in brief disapproval when she saw me but refrained from comment. She was herself a bit disheveled and still wearing two hundred dollar sweats (no sweat obvious, however). His Excellency the butler came in with a tray full of silver service and finger sandwiches and was dismissed until called.

Agnes had not spoken and did not until she had poured our tea. I waited, no point in calling down her thunder until she was ready to unleash it. Her first words were remarkably calm. Apparently Altamor P.D. had not yet talked to her.

"What have you to say for yourself? Did Betty Cash tell you anything?"

"Betty Cash had nothing to say. I found her dead on Monday morning. I thought you knew, it was in the papers."

Agnes choked on her tea. Drying her face with her napkin, she said, ""You found her dead? I read that she was dead and murder was suspected but there wasn't a word about your involvement. Where have you been? Hiding? Why? Did you kill her? Did she really have the Rembrandt?"

I saw that the only way to deal with her was to tell her the whole story, starting with my conversation with Dolly Hack. I wondered silently how she had recognized Mrs. Broward in the news item as Betty Cash. When Agnes heard that the painting had disappeared, gone from the frame and probably with the murderer, her face went stiff and cold. She leaped from her chair and started to pace. She grew so pale that her carefully applied makeup stood out in patches on her white cheeks and lips. When her color returned, it was the red of rage.

"That bitch! That bitch!" she almost screamed. "She called me two weeks ago and wanted to negotiate again; poor-mouthed up a storm, fallen on hard times she said; offered me Adrian's picture for a thousand dollars, said she'd call back as soon as she had her ducks in a row. When I asked what ducks, she just giggled and hung up."

"Did you get an impression she was shopping the picture around? Had other offers, maybe?"

By a tremendous effort of will, Agnes regained her poise and her seat. Her hand shook as she took up her teacup but otherwise she was in control of her emotions.

"Why didn't you tell me she had contacted you?" I scolded.

"What could you do? She didn't give me an address or phone number. I thought if she was willing to deal, I could handle it."

I wondered if there were more to all of this than Agnes wanted me to know. Maybe Betty had called Agnes a week, not two weeks, ago; maybe she had given Agnes an address. It would be just like Agnes to send a henchman, Wicker perhaps, to follow through. Someone like Wicker might be so tempted by two million dollars worth of painting that a hasty swipe to put Betty Cash down, followed by a bed pillow crammed over her nose and mouth, was a risk worth taking. Wicker would have known that the frame probably held the Rembrandt. I was reasonably confident that the Rembrandt was not back in Agnes's hands. If it were, a smug smile would surely have leaked through her lies and evasions. What if her fury was for her cats-paw, and not for

Betty? Had the cats-paw reneged on a deal with Agnes? Holding the painting for ransom? Looking for a buyer?

I left as soon as Agnes had emptied the plate of finger sandwiches. I wondered at her greed. Real hunger or displacement activity? But she hadn't dismissed my services and I had a lot more to think about.

❧ 18 ❧

When I got home, Amos Puckett's limo was parked at the curb and Amos was conferring with Zulu. He interrupted the conference to come hastily to meet me.

"Ms. Crenshaw. I am so glad to see you. Mama has been driving me up the wall for word of you."

"Dear me!" I replied. "Why?"

"Just before she fell, she took a very important phone message for you, and in the subsequent flurry forgot to tell you. She refuses to give the message to a third party, insists you are the only one who should hear it. Would you be so kind as to visit her and put her mind at ease?"

"Of course. Where is she now? And how is she getting along?"

Amos scribbled the address of the Meadowlands Convalescent Home on the back of a business card. Mrs. Puckett was doing as well as could be expected and would enjoy a visitor, but me especially.

"Seeing you and discharging her responsibility for that phone message will probably be better than medication to put her mind and body at rest. Her anxiety has me worried."

I promised to visit tomorrow and he resumed his interview with Zulu. The House phone rang, and I answered it to spare Amos and Zulu another interruption. It was Ben, all in a tizzy.

"Are you finally back in the land of the living?" he demanded. "I've tried day after day to reach you. Bertha at the Museum gave me this number today...."

I placated him with my cell phone number and told him to call back in five minutes when I would be in the privacy of my apartment. I wondered why he was so fussed. Was he going to call off our date? I hoped not. After the events of this week, I could use a agreeable interlude with a charming male companion.

As it turned out, he had talked with Jonesy on Monday, learned I intended to drop out of sight for a few days, and started to worry.

"Why would you worry?" I asked.

His answer was short on specifics. "Jonesy told me your investigation had taken an ugly turn and knowing you had seen Dolly Hack, I suspected trouble. Maybe we should talk about my special interest in your investigation."

"Why in the world should you have a special interest in what I'm doing?"

"You'll understand when we talk. I'll fill you in at dinner. Tomorrow, wear casual clothes because I want to treat you to the best barbecued ribs this side of the Mississippi. After the finger lickin' is over, we might take in a classic movie at the Cinema Center. They're showing *High Noon.* "

Refusing to say more, he left me acutely curious. "Wait and see," he insisted. He was still out of town but expected to return early Saturday afternoon and would pick me up at 5 P.M. Our conversation ended, I was suddenly bone tired and headed for a hot soak in the bathtub. I was in bed by 8 and slept through till 8 A.M.

After a morning at the Museum I went to see Mrs. Puckett. The campus of Meadowlands Convalescent Home was handsomely landscaped and studded with big trees; it smelled of money, an odor emphasized by elegantly furnished common rooms populated by well-dressed ambulatory patients. The building was a two-story hollow square surrounding a lovely interior garden. I was directed down a long hall to the orthopedic unit to find Mrs. Puckett. Stopping to look in at the open door of her room, I saw her, eyes closed peacefully, lying under neatly smoothed covers, her face as white as her hair and the pillow case under her head. I tiptoed in with the pot of brilliantly yellow lantana I had purchased at a florist on the way. At the slight noise I made as I set it down, Mrs. Puckett's eyes flew open in instant recognition. Her welcome was as quick.

"Oh, Miss Crenshaw, I am so glad to see you. This place is so boring. The only excitement is a bath and a change of bed linens, or a meal tray. There's television but it's boring too. So far you and Amos are my only visitors. My rehab exercises start on Monday; I'm looking forward to them to break up the time if they don't break me up first."

She ran out of breath and pent up frustration at the same time.

"Mrs. Puckett, you seem pretty lively. I was afraid you would be too sleepy to enjoy a visit."

"Oh, no. I made them quit the pain medication. I want to get along without it. The doctor said I could have it whenever I thought I needed it. I hate feeling dopey, and I wanted especially to be bright when you came. Amos said he told you I had to see you."

"Yes, he mentioned a phone message that was preying on your mind. I'm sure it was nothing important."

"Oh, yes, it was. Important and urgent. A man called just a few minutes before I fell but then everything turned topsy-turvy and I didn't remember to tell you. I can't thank you enough for all you did for me that Sunday afternoon. Amos told me you stayed right by my side until he got there. Bless you for your kindness. Where was I?"

"You were telling me about the phone message," I prompted.

"Yes, well, it was a man and the message was 'Fifteen hundred cash and it's yours.' I asked him twice for his name but all he said was "Tell her Jay Double, she'll know. I got to go.' I tried to tell him you would be back any minute or that I could take his number for you to return the call. But he just said again 'I got to go' and hung up. I think I was looking for a pencil and pad to write down the message when I fell. He spoke so urgently it's been worrying me ever since. Where were you that Amos couldn't catch you until yesterday?"

I gave her a quick summary of my vacation at the Retreat House. She nodded in approval, saying that I and the students all worked too hard and needed time off. But her energy was fading and I patted her hand, as thin and bony as a bird's claw, to bid her farewell. I came away with a new puzzle. Jay Double, fifteen hundred cash. Cash might mean Betty Cash or a payoff, or both. Fifteen hundred seemed to resonate with the thousand dollars Betty had solicited from Agnes. Jay Double—someone I would know. I racked my brain on the way back to my office. Jonesy was in his office and I stopped in to bring him up to date on my encounters with Altamor police and Agnes Emmons. With a twinkle in his eye he complimented me on my civic conscience and said he hoped I would not regret it.

"What's next on your agenda?" he asked. "I hope you're not quitting. Agnes still doesn't have her painting back and you have her advance."

"No, I'm not quitting! In fact, I may have a new lead."

And I told him of the message Mrs. Puckett had just relayed. I was pretty sure the combination of a number and the word "cash" referred to something Jay Double knew about the Object. Jonesy was no help in guessing the identity of Jay Double but he again counseled me to wait out the police investigation of Betty Cash's murder. I left the Museum for dinner at the Commons and afterwards picked up a newspaper at the cashier's stand. Once home I excised the ad supplement from the paper in order to make it more easily read as I sprawled on my lumpy bed. The OpEd page caught my attention with a cartoon captioned "What's Dubya gonna deny next?" Of course! I sat bolt upright. The man had told Mrs. Puckett Jay Double **U!** J.W., John Wicker. I immediately punched in his number on my cell phone but had no answer. My mind raced furiously to a potentially ill-founded conclusion, a scenario in which Betty Cash, upping the ante beyond the thousand dollars she asked of Agnes, had got in touch with John Wicker and asked him to negotiate for fifteen hundred, and Wicker, still unwilling to do business with Betty or Agnes, had downloaded a new clue to me. Whether or not I was operating on a false premise, I wasn't at a dead end after all.

❧ 19 ❧

Dinner with Ben was delightful. He delivered on his boast of the best ribs west of the Mississippi. Although my geographic experience with barbecued ribs was limited, I could agree on the excellence of those on the large platter in front of us. We ate our way happily through them and a big bowl of coleslaw, then repaired to a nearby coffee house and a table in a remote corner. I told Ben it was time to deliver on his promise to clear up his mystery. He reached over, took my hand, then began with an apology.

"I'm probably going to make you mad and I'm sorry. But I have to admit our encounter at the Theta Pi bash was no accident. I conspired with Jonesy to be there because I wanted to meet you and probe your recent activities."

"Why should you want to know about my activities? What business of yours could they possibly be?" I was miffed and my tone of voice clearly conveyed my irritation.

"They started to become my business when you called on John Wicker and went on to dog Al Grover and to see Dolly Hack. We started surveillance over your comings and goings after you called on Dolly. I'm sorry…."

Now I was mad! I half-rose and tried to pull my hand away from Ben but he tightened his warm grasp and I had to yield. I wanted to get up and flounce out but I confess I also wanted to hear the other shoe drop. A temper tantrum wouldn't get me more information so I settled grudgingly back onto my chair. Ben began an explanation, measuring his words and cryptic phrases.

"The government agency I work for has an ongoing investigation into an enormous fraud. Al Grover, Dolly Hack, and Betty Cash are—were— minor players. Contacting them made you a person of interest and learning what you were after became important to my professional interest. Unfortunately or fortunately, meeting you fired my personal interest. I think you're a really neat lady. You're pretty, smart, cultivated, all the things I admire in a female, and I like you, a lot. The reason I'm confiding in you now is that I like you too much to continue sailing under false colors. I can't tell you a whole story. Probably I'm violating my ethics to tell you this much, but the murder of Betty Cash has introduced a whole new set of issues, some of them boding serious danger for you. I have to ask you to trust me, to share the facts you have gathered, to confide your impressions and opinions. Will you?"

I managed to get my hand free from his. I needed to break the physical connection in order to get my thoughts organized. As I looked up into Ben's face, his eyes now shadowed with his concern, I wanted with all my heart to trust him. What I had shared with Jonesy was my collection of day-to-day scraps of fact. He and I had not discussed those scraps, speculated, or built logical scenarios from them. I yearned for a knowledgeable confidant with whom to mull over my current mishmash of data. I hoped for an confidant with powerful connections to more information. I wanted a potential resolution to my quest for Giovane. Was Ben a key to my goal? I resolved to gamble, but first I challenged him.

"How do I know you are what you claim to be? Do you have a badge, or a certificate, or an official superior with whom I can check references?"

He grinned, reached for his wallet, and pushed it across the table at me. I opened it on a thin gold shield bearing a U.S. Treasury logo; on the obverse his name and a number were engraved below a ceramic image. I also found credit cards and a perfectly ordinary driver's license with his name and photo. I closed the wallet and pushed it back. He nodded,

"You do well to check on me. I can't give you references because my superiors would be very upset to learn I had disclosed myself to a civilian. Maybe after I know what you know, I can tell them without risk of discipline. How about it?"

I gave in to his probing and started the story with my first encounter with Agnes Cathcart DeWitt Emmons. As it became obvious we needed to examine a lot of documentation, Ben asked, "Can we go to your office at the Museum? Privacy is called for, I think. My memory is not fault-free and the sequence of your information is just confusing enough to mandate an *aide memoire*."

Sure, I said, and we were soon ensconced at my desk with dossiers and the log of my notes in front of us. The museum was closed, the lighting dim. High ceilings and bare floors of the galleries echoed with the footsteps of the guards on their rounds. It was a bit eerie but the guards were accustomed to my nocturnal work hours and they accepted Ben on my say-so. The photos of Giovane and Adrian Cash illustrated the narration of my quest and the mass of handwritten and typed reports. Ben commented on Giovane.

"An arresting face and an arresting pose. A sexy tease, isn't he? I can understand the fascination the painting exerts on Agnes and you and even on Adrian Cash. Sticking that photo of himself over the painting was something of a salute to the painted face. He strove to be a co-conspirator in Giovane's joke."

I was beginning to appreciate even more the mystique of Giovane. I ached to get that painting back! My determination grew as Ben and I constructed and discussed the logic of my findings and my hope increased that Ben's connections would facilitate a successful conclusion to my search. It was 4 A.M. before we had gone through everything. Ben and I were both bleary-eyed and he had writer's cramp besides. He must have learned to write minuscule from poring over medieval manuscripts. At any rate, I found his notes illegible; tiny script and abstruse abbreviations encoded the content. I locked up all the stuff in Jonesy's safe. Somehow analyzing and organizing it seemed to make it more vulnerable. Ben drove me home and promised to call later in the day. I tumbled into bed fully dressed and fell instantly and deeply into sleep.

🌤 20 🌤

It was noon before I woke. I lolled in bed for another hour, pondering what Ben and I had talked about. I realized at last that I had told him a whole lot more than he had told me. Doubts were rising in my mind. Was that badge legitimate? Was Ben a resource or a hindrance, competitor or colleague, in my search for Giovane? Was I letting my liking for the man blind me to consideration that he might have a hidden agenda? I had only met him two weeks ago. Did I know him? Had I trusted him too soon? Were the scraps he had let fall about his big fraud investigation sufficiently adequate or credible to dispel my doubts? I finally got up, made coffee, and ate cold cereal and a banana. I hunted up Zulu with my rent check in hand and found her doing accounts downstairs at Mrs. Puckett's desk. She was humming cheerfully as she logged in the week's receipts and expenditures. She allowed me an unscheduled shower and afterwards, dressed for the day, I headed for the Student Commons to pick up a Sunday paper. I scanned the headlines, dumped a humongous wad of advertising into the Commons's trash cans, and took the rest home to read at leisure. Zulu caught me at the door.

"Your Mom called. She sounded upset, she said she needs to talk to you. Wanted to know if you would you call her at home or come."

I thanked her and continued upstairs, fighting the urge to ignore the message but finally yielding and punching the buttons on the cell phone. Momma's voice was choked with sobs when she answered.

"Zima? Is it you? Oh, Zima, I'm in so much trouble. Your dad had a stroke last night. We got him to the hospital and the doctors say it's bad. He's in ICU. I'm afraid he'll die without saying good-bye to you. Won't you put aside your vexation with us and go to see him? The hours for family are 4 to 5 and only one at a time can go to the bedside. Oh, Zima, please...." Her sobs drowned out the rest of her news.

"All right, Mom. I'll go. Stop crying. Tell me. How he is affected? Is he conscious? Can he walk? Talk? What did the doctors say about recovery?"

"His eyes are open and when he looked at me, I thought he knew me. But me and Peter had to drag him to the car. The orderlies at the hospital got him out and on a cart. He didn't try to help at all. He didn't talk to me or to the doctor, just sort of gargled in his throat. The doctor said they couldn't give a pro-, prog-, prag-, something -nosis...."

I supplied the word "prognosis" and urged her on.

She continued, saying "They have to have the results of a whole bunch of tests. I don't understand them but Peter says MRI and CAT scans and ultrasounds are what the doctors are talking about. They say the Medicare will take care of everything. I remembered to take all the papers with me, I didn't fall apart until after they had him in the ICU. Now I can't seem to stop crying."

I tried to soothe her with platitudes and she seemed more in control of her emotions by the time we disconnected. Ben called around two o'clock; he took my news with aplomb and said he would call again.

"Let's just put our projects on hold until you are free to pursue them. I'll work on a few leads I can follow and the next time we meet we can evaluate them together. Just hang in there in the meantime."

Sure, I'd hang in there. What else could I do? I wished I could put a name to the feelings I was having about Dad's condition. I cared and hated it that I cared. Caring from love? Hardly, but maybe from concern for Mom. What if Dad died? Would his pension stop? What would Mom live on? Peter's pittance wouldn't carry the two of them. I should look into the pension coverage, maybe there was provision for a widow. I felt suddenly responsible for them. I was young, healthy, competent, I would have to take charge. Or would I? Take charge or meddle? I valued my independence. If Dad was out of the picture, I would have to work out a new relationship with Mom. My head in a muddle, I changed clothes to an outfit suited to a hospital visit and left. I was at the ICU reception desk at exactly 4 P.M. A singularly inept woman—white-haired, wearing a pink smock, obviously a volunteer—rummaged through a stack of forms. She finally found one and held it up in triumph.

"Edgar Crenshaw? Is he the one? Well, here it says Room B-3, visitors limited to members of the family. Oh, you are the daughter? OK. You're allowed 10 minutes at the bedside. Through that door, Room B-3 is in there somewhere. Ask a nurse. Have a nice day."

Irritation and impatience with her inefficiency, stupidity, rudeness, and carelessness welled up but I swallowed my aggravation and decided to accept them with good grace. These people were working in the best interests of my dad and a lot of other patients; I would not find fault with their minor failings. Inside the ICU I found a pleasant welcome and courteous directions to Room B-3. The nurses went about their duties soft-footed and spoke to one another and the patients in hushed tones. Dad lay motionless, eyes closed, covered to the chin, a fluid drip line snaking under the covers presumably to his hand or arm. His scanty fluff of hair and bushy eyebrows emphasized the shape of his head against the pillow and the ashen white of his normally ruddy cheeks. When I looked down at him and spoke, his eyes opened and focused on me. In them I read fear, bewilderment, surprise. It came as a revelation that I understood his state of mind. He was used to being boss, in charge, on top, and now he lay helpless and perhaps hopeless. I was moved to pity and bent to place a kiss on his forehead. I couldn't remember ever kissing my father. Maybe reconciliation could begin in pity, if it didn't come too late, that is. I murmured reassurances that Dad seemed to hear and understand. As surprise in his gaze faded, anxiety and bewilderment persisted. I unearthed his free hand from the covers and spent the remainder of my 10 minutes holding and stroking it. It lay flaccid and unresponsive in my hand but I thought Dad's eyes recognized a benign intent. I wondered what was going through his mind. Was he remembering the quarrels and bickering as I was? We had never made up that I remembered, instead had simply gone on from one clash to the next.

As I returned to the reception room, Mom was waiting to go in. She wore face powder, lipstick, cologne, and her newest Sunday dress. She had clothed herself in bravery to confront this disaster in her life. I hugged her and said, "I think he knew me, even though he didn't move or speak."

Her face puckered up but she remembered her makeup and heroically suppressed her tears with a weak smile and turned to go through the door to the ICU. The intern on duty at the nursing station had waffled answers to my questions, unwilling to commit to anything more than the official diagnosis: a hemorrhagic stroke, no longer bleeding. He gave me the name of the neurologist in charge of the case and told me to expect her to call a conference with family members when the medical picture had stabilized. I had him add my telephone numbers to Dad's chart (Mom only knew the Puckett House number). I passed by the hospital cafeteria on my way out and glanced in to glimpse Peter hunched over a tray loaded with fried chicken, mashed potatoes and gravy, and two kinds of cake. I did not turn aside to greet him.

I drove home with a lot of crazy thoughts churning in my brain. Selfish thoughts surfaced most often. Dad's stroke was likely to interfere big time with the search for Giovane and my newly won independence of the Crenshaws. I might be obliged to move back home to look after Mom. Angrily I refused to consider looking after Peter. If Dad survived, I wondered about rehab facilities, nursing home care, cost of medications. Of course, if he didn't survive, then …. Buried in my thoughts I ran a stop light, fortunately without consequences, woke up with a start to force myself to stop thinking, and turned up the volume on the radio. A jazz program blared. I hate jazz, but too cranky to change the station, I simply concentrated on driving and disliking what I was hearing.

❧ 21 ❧

I drove on to the campus and parked in the Museum lot. The weather was beautiful. The bright blue October sky was fringed with trailing white cirrus clouds; the hardwoods lining the drives were brilliant with color startling against the lawns still green. I sat in the car with the windows open, luxuriating in the balmy breeze blowing through it. I was taking time to think over my current circumstances. The realization dawned on me that my visit to the Retreat House, the visit I had been calling a vacation, was truly only an escape from the horror of Betty Cash's murder. Time at the House had not resolved any of my deep-seated problems. It had done no more than soothe the superficial stresses of my hunt for Giovane. Dad's stroke was a different matter; it reopened the Pandora's box of my childhood that I thought I had closed when I moved out on the family. I was no self-directed psychologist but now I was forced by developments to think about the tortuously interlocking threads of resentment and yes, *hate* that had scarred my youth.

I suppose it had started with the manifest favoritism my mother and father had lavished on Peter. In their minds he was the important child, the eldest, the smartest, the most talented, the most worthy of their attention and affection. In my mind he was cruel and abusive, taking every opportunity when unobserved by adults to slap or poke me or to humiliate me. He pushed me into the mud and then told Mom I had waded in it deliberately. He pulled my pants down in front of the neighbor kids and led the jeers and laughter. I brought home straight A grade cards that were received without comment; Peter's cards were studded with Ds and Cs but Mom and Dad praised him for "doing his best" and "better than last time." At the dinner table, Mom put the tenderest pieces of meat, or biggest slices of cake with the most icing on Dad's and Peter's plates. There was always enough for them to have dibs on second helpings of the tastiest dishes. What they didn't want, I could have.

By the time I went to high school, I had learned to look out for myself. I ignored Peter's insults and cheap shots, I overlooked Mom's catering to Peter, and I shrugged off Dad's lack of interest in me and my accomplishments. I stopped quarreling at home, gritted my teeth, swallowed my resentments, and got on with my life. I set myself to win the esteem of teachers, mentors, and other adults in my life. My success in college was due to kindly guidance from them and hard work on my part. Operating inside a shell of calculated indifference, I shared neither failures nor achievements with my family. I substituted academic success for the shortcomings of my home life. And I pulled it off rather well. Now I was realizing the price of my isolation from them and a need to extend at least undemanding tolerance, at most reconciliation. All the same, I saw no value in reconciling with Peter. His laziness repelled me. His career consisted of sitting in front of the TV, munching snack foods, or hanging out with his cronies at the neighborhood bar. Despite the dribble of money his disability payments brought into the house, he had sponged off Dad for years. The injury for which he was being compensated became a handicap only when he found it convenient. He displayed a real talent for acting when he was getting psyched up for his annual visit to the orthopedist. I hated his hypocrisy!

When I thought about Mom, it was with compassion. I felt sorry for her and now I regretted I had not been kinder to her, more understanding while I was practicing detachment from the men in the house. I remembered the wedding picture on the mantel: Mom, a gauzy veil floating from her crown of fresh flowers, smooth cheeks, wide innocent eyes, a pretty girl in an elegant white lace dress. I remembered her the day I decided to leave home: worry wrinkles around tired eyes, hair untidy, wearing a grubby apron over a faded print dress and run-over shoes. A daughter shouldn't have to feel sorry for her mother; there should be a warmer, deeper emotion. Now I wondered if her attitude to me as I grew up was to mollify Dad, to keep her and my profile low enough so as to minimize as much conflict as possible. I knew that Dad's frequent response to a request for household money was a slap or a cuff. Submission was probably the tactful way for her to live with him.

Sitting there in that car, remembering the slings and arrows my family life had fired at me, I came to an epiphany. Left on my own to deal with my juvenile stresses, I had mistakenly chosen to wall my emotions and feelings off from them. I consciously constructed a parallel life, one in which I physically remained in the Crenshaw house but psychologically outside the Crenshaw family. My choice had perhaps kept me from drug or alcohol addictions or mental meltdowns or antisocial behaviors, but tearing down the wall now forced me to face the cost of a dysfunctional relationship with my family. Of course, recognizing it provided no insight to correcting it; even analyzing it would probably be fruitless. Nevertheless, I could resolve to practice tolerance and pretend caring. Hadn't it been said "Pretending can make it so"? I got out of the car, committed to trying.

I made a brief visit to my office, watched the guards shoo a straggle of visitors from the galleries, and after the doors were locked, walked around viewing my favorite exhibits and turning off lights. I loved the dim peacefulness of this hour in the Museum. I picked up the visitor's log and read the visitor's comments. I was always delighted with expressions of delight and pleasure and desolated by criticism. Today, Granville Harris had found the lighting over our Monet "absolutely abominable." One shaky signature deplored the scantiness of Lincoln memorabilia. I would plan to follow up on those comments tomorrow. Now I was going to my light blue apartment, exhausted by introspection, and have a toasted cheese sandwich and a bowl of tomato soup.

❧ 22 ❧

In the event, Ben was calling as I unlocked my door and inviting me out to dine. His invitation revived me and I accepted with alacrity. We went to a pleasant little tea-roomish place for broiled chicken breast sauced with creamed peas, a splendid green salad, a heavenly cheesecake, and coffee. Ben asked politely after my father and listened to some of my worries. He fastened on one of them with a question.

"Did your father have life insurance or mortgage insurance? If he should die, your mother might be in better circumstances than you imagine. If you would sit down with your mother and talk over things like that, she would probably value a confidante at a time like this and you might achieve some peace of mind, don't you think?"

He was right. On Monday, I called Mom and asked her to lunch with me before she went to the hospital. When I picked her up, she had again donned makeup and her best dress. Only the lingering redness of her eyelids told the story of tears shed in lonely hours at home. I took her to Beverley's, a quiet, rather elegant restaurant with soft music, attractive furnishings, and lovely potted plants. I could see she was intimidated by the menu until she realized the prices were modest. To justify never eating out, Dad made a practice to rail at high prices and overdone décor of popular restaurants.

Timidly she asked, "What's good?"

She drew a long breath of relief when I recommended the special, chicken salad on a croissant at 5.99, and suggested iced tea. She ate with real relish; I suspected she had kept Peter fed but not herself since Dad was in the hospital. We chatted about trivia: the asters at their peak in the back yard, a family of goldfinches that patronized the feeder outside the kitchen window, the price of meat at the local supermarket.

"Mom," I finally asked a question that wasn't trivial, "If Dad doesn't make it, how will you be fixed? Is the mortgage paid off? Does he have life insurance?"

She brightened, "Oh, yes, we paid off the mortgage the year you finished high school. And Ed has a $100,000 policy. If you are worrying about me, don't. Your dad left business for the household to me and everything is paid up. There are some government bonds; there's money in the savings account. Ed never went to high school, you know. He felt my certificate from business college qualified me to handle our financial affairs. He always said he would earn the money and I could manage it."

Makeup or not, tears spilled over her cheeks. "But he was so tight, he wouldn't let me spend it on anything he considered frivolous. After he retired he was tighter than ever, used to fuss about the grocery bills and Girl Scout cookies. He didn't have much else to do. Oh, now, I've messed up my face."

She fumbled in her purse for tissues and blew her nose. "Your dad wasn't a bad man, he was always a good provider, that was his way of caring for us, he didn't know any other way. He was often so frustrated being held back at his job and his inability to speak proper English, he either didn't say anything at all or he hit out." She broke down completely.

I guided her to the rest room. She cried herself out then bathed her face in cold water.

"I didn't think you would care about him or me," she said. "You left without a word and never called or wrote."

I had no answer. Finally she squared her shoulders, glanced at her watch, and said we had better get going if we were to meet with the neurologist at three.

The neurologist was a diminutive Asian woman with an ageless Asian face, even though a good many years had marked her skinny fingers and wrinkled hands. Dr. Liang sat Mom and me down in a conference room, opened a fat folder of test results, and politely opened the conversation.

"Mrs. Crenshaw, Miss Crenshaw, I'm afraid I have not good news for you. Mr. Edgar has had a very serious hemorrhagic cranial event and is not responding well to our efforts to treat him. I very much doubt he will ever speak again. He may recover limited motion in his hands and arms but not enough to feed or attend to himself. I have established a degree of communication with him; he can blink twice for no and once for yes. When I phrased the questions just right, his blinks told me that he has no pain, that the food he is given is satisfactory, that he prefers coffee to soda. He seems still to possess mentation, to what degree I cannot say. The full extent of brain competency will have to be determined over time."

"What next?" I asked.

"If the hemorrhage recurs, death is assured. If not, he will need to be placed in a facility for total care, for how long I cannot say. The damage to the brain appears so extensive that rehabilitation is unlikely. Bedsores and inanition are to be expected and patients such as he are acutely vulnerable to pneumonia. An encouraging prognosis for long term survival is tentative at best. I am sorry to tell you these things but it is best that you know them. You can then adjust better to future circumstances."

Mom sat straight-backed and dry-eyed to hear what Dr. Liang had to say. When it seemed that everything had been said, she mustered her dignity, rose, shook the doctor's hand, and left the room. I followed. It was 4 P.M. and Mom went on in to visit Dad. I waited until she came out and told me she wanted to be taken home. Her jaw was firm set and her eyes still dry. We didn't talk on the way home and she didn't invite me in. She went up the walk and porch stair with steady steps. My heart was breaking. Dad was a lost cause; Mom was dealing with that fact with courage I never knew she had. It goes to show, you never know the steel that lies beneath the skin.

❧ 23 ❧

The following week at the Museum was wild. Leslie Heaver was mounting an exhibit dubbed *18th Century Times*, working with a collection of timepieces loaned by an 85-year-old eccentric. With the deadline for the opening looming, Les came down with a virulent strep throat and Jonesy had to take over. He begged me to help him out and we worked 12-hour days. Our generous elderly patron was a crank, to put it kindly, and we had to nurse his whims and quirks day in and day out. I managed to get to the hospital two or three times; Dad's condition didn't vary and he was due to be moved to the hospice on Saturday. Mom visited every day and was allowed to sit with him for as long as she wished. On Friday late in the afternoon she called to tell me Dad wasn't expected to survive the night; his brain was bleeding again. Jonesy urged me to leave; I arrived at Dad's bedside minutes after he had been pronounced dead. When I looked at him, I saw that death had wiped the marks of age and illness from his face, leaving his features as clean and sharp as the profile on a newly minted coin. He looked again like the handsome lad in the wedding picture on the mantel. I bent briefly and kissed his brow in farewell. Mom, face set, eyes dry, picked up her purse and magazine and taking my arm, led me out of the room. My scanty tears were for her. She calmly signed the necessary papers and asked me to drive her home. When I asked what else I should do, she said,

"All the arrangements are made. I alerted Myers Mortuary three days ago. There won't be a viewing, just a memorial service. I'll have Mr. Lacey, that lay preacher that lives next to us, hold it Sunday afternoon at his church. We bought our cemetery plot years ago. The church ladies will serve a collation. I don't expect many guests. Now, if you don't mind, stop by the bar so I can tell Peter Dad's gone."

Her calm was almost frightening, but then I reflected that she had undoubtedly done her grieving in those hours she had spent with him before he died. I asked again what I could do for her and she said,

"Nothing, dear. Although I may ask you tomorrow to drive me somewhere if I can't get Peter to do it. Go back to your work for now and we'll sit down Sunday evening and talk things out."

Back at my office I found a message from Ben and a number to return his call. He expressed his condolences in well-chosen words and sincere tones. He asked how the exhibit was coming and I was pleased to say it would open on time on Sunday, Jonesy presiding.

Allowing just a slight edge of sarcasm to creep into my voice, I asked, "Do you think we could get together on Monday or Tuesday to get our project back on track? Or will you be out of town again?"

Ben's reply surprised me. "I'll see you at the funeral and we'll make our plans then. In the meantime, spend as much time as your mom needs to get through this."

"Well, I get a distinct impression she doesn't really want me underfoot. But I can be useful as a driver for her. Peter acts like Dad was somebody else's father and husband, a stranger. Maybe it's his way of dealing with death or maybe he just doesn't care. My guess it's the latter."

Ben ignored my bitterness and his inquiry into the time and location of the service changed the subject. When he signed off I got to work on some last minute details of the exhibit.

On Sunday our minister neighbor held a very nice service at the New Covenant Chapel. He hadn't known Dad, and our family had never been religious, so he strung together a lot of Bible readings while his wife played a soft piano background. As we expected, the congregation was skimpy: a few neighbors, Ben, Jonesy who had skipped out on the *Times* opening, Zulu, Juan, and to my surprise, Amos Puckett. Amos expressed his mother's condolences at length. Peter appeared briefly, spreading himself over a back pew which creaked under his weight. He didn't follow the cortege to the cemetery and Mom and I stood alone as the casket was lowered into the ground. When she and I were back home later, facing one another over the kitchen table and cups of hot coffee, I voiced my fears for her future.

"Zima, dear, you should have no fears for me. All of the property is in both Ed's and my name, the will assigns everything to the surviving spouse, and that's me. The insurance is in order. I have in mind to sell this house and take a small condominium in the Coventry Cove development just down the street. I haven't driven for many years but I thought I would take lessons and make myself independent. Ed's car is only three years old…"

I interrupted her to ask, "What about Peter?"

A shadow passed over her face, but her answer came quickly. "I've already told him my plans and that there wasn't room for him in my new place. He didn't take it well. It's too bad he feels rejected, but you know as well as I do that I've waited on him hand and foot for years and I'm tired of it. I checked on his disability allowance and there's enough for him to live on, as long as he doesn't hire a maid and butler!"

She laughed without genuine humor, then went on,

"I'd like you to pick out any household things you might want when I break up housekeeping. Most of the stuff is old and shabby but the china that belonged to Ed's mother and the platform rocker that was my grandmother's are nice. Oh, Zima, I feel like I'm beginning a new life. I'll miss Ed, we were married for 38 years, but in these last years he was more a habit than a husband. Our life together was never easy and it got harder when he retired. Now I feel freed, adventurous, energetic. I don't know how to express it. I hope I'll see more of you when I'm settled in Coventry Cove; I took an option on a unit with a small guest room. You might come for an overnight once in a while."

When I left, I went away happy and relieved. Not only was there one of my family to whom I was fully reconciled, that one was in charge of her life and enjoying the future it promised.

❧ 24 ❧

Ben and I had made a date for breakfast at the Student Commons. Neither the ambience nor the cuisine was elegant but the baked goods were tasty and the coffee was hot. We went from there to my office at the Museum and hauled out the Giovane file from Jonesy's safe in order to review a few points.

"I went to look up John Wicker," Ben volunteered. "The address you had was swept clean. Well, not clean, the correct word is empty. A demolition order was posted on the front wall of the building. The super still in residence saw Wicker leaving the building empty-handed two weeks ago, the day before he left his message at the Puckett House, but no one saw him move out. The taxi driver who picked him up said he dropped him at Prospect Park. No sign of him since, no report of a missing person. The address on his P.I. license is that empty office. His only phone was the one in that derelict office, not even a cell phone on record. A team from my agency is hard at work tracing his background and possible fate."

"Too bad they're not working on Betty Cash," I said sourly.

"Oh, but they are," Ben retorted. "Hand in glove with Rodriguez and the Altamor P.D. Everything is very hush-hush but connections among Betty, Dolly Mead, Al Grover, and J.R. Wicker are emerging. Not only that, their connection to the perpetrators of the fraud I spoke of is beginning to make sense."

"Well, it may make sense to your team, but none of its efforts seem likely to get me any closer to the Giovane. I owe Agnes Emmons that missing painting or a damn good reason why she can't have it back!"

"If it's any comfort, I've wangled permission to fill in the background of the task force's current work for you and an invitation to sit in on its next meeting. There's been a bureaucratic fruit-basket upset and more open minds are now in the seats of power, if you don't mind horribly scrambled metaphors. Anyway, you must understand that everything you will learn is deadly secret because the chain of evidence is still missing critical links. My new bosses thought you could contribute usefully to their case. Are you willing to swear to silence?"

"Scout's honor! Shoot! I'm all ears."

"Can you be all ears on a bench under a tree over by the tennis courts?"

Sure, I said and off we went after locking the office door. Like a comic opera conspirator in a B-movie, Ben scanned east, west, north, and south before beginning, then grew serious.

"You've heard of Anchron, major purveyor of energy resources to municipal governments, with holdings in the billions and until this past year an unblemished reputation in financial circles for ethical business practices. A crack in its façade became known to the Treasury Department by way of a whistle blower, whose offended conscience had overcome his company loyalty. Treasury immediately swung into action but so far has managed to keep a lid on the nature of the problem.

116

Treasury and the Anchron board hope to keep the scandal quiet until radical action taken in a single division can forestall total collapse. If Anchron crashes, millions of taxpayer dollars and investors' funds will go up in smoke. "

"That's big, all right. But what *is* the nature of the problem?"

"Transfers of significant amounts of non-existent Anchron stock to foreign companies in third world countries struggling to achieve economic development, the purchases backed and the value guaranteed by the U.S. Government under an obscure provision of an law enacted in the 80s."

"In this day and age, aren't transfers all done electronically? How can non-existent stock be transferred by that means? Isn't there a trail in some computer somewhere?"

"Yes and no. There's an electronic trail that appears to legitimize the transfers, but the money paid for the stock has gone astray. It seems that certain Anchron officials getting complaints from companies in Africa about delays in electronic receipt placated them with counterfeit paper certificates, which those companies subsequently used to secure large loans from European banks. There are some three hundred million dollars worth of fraudulent stock out there. If this scam, maybe skim is a better word, becomes known before the perpetrators are detained, Anchron will crash. A lot of Americans will lose their investments and pay again in taxes since American law makes the United States government responsible for the losses. Already shaky African governments may crash as well."

"I don't really understand. How do such small fish as Betty and her pals figure in the scam? Of course, the officials pulling this stunt have been squirreling away money by wire in Caribbean Islands. Undoubtedly the remarkable prosperity that they display and the diligence of your people will disclose the offshore accounts, but I can't see any evidence that Betty's crowd has profited from those shenanigans."

"This is how Betty's crowd is involved. The whistle blower happened to know the names of three couriers trusted to travel with fraudulent certificates in their brief cases. Even as we speak, airline records are being scoured for ticketing dates and destinations for Evan Hunter, Elizabeth Cady, and Mary Lou Evans. Receipt of certificates at a dozen or so African companies at selected destinations has been verified. The faces of Al, Betty, and Dolly are readily identified on surveillance tapes of airport boarding areas on the dates of tickets issued to their aliases. We believe they were recruited as couriers with promises of big payoffs when the project came to an end, while the delay in the payoffs was explained as critical to avoiding premature detection of the caper."

"So, it's conceivable that an attempt to blackmail bigwigs may have led to Betty's murder, but the painting...? How can the painting's disappearance be explained?"

"At the moment, I don't think it can. We need more information. I'm told that the investigators have got the goods on the two guys who have been robbing the till and are about to arrest them. But nabbing them won't necessarily clear up the fate of the painting, will it?"

"Let's go in. Hearing nothing but bad news makes this bench too hard for me to sit on any longer," I said peevishly.

Ben laughed and made some crack about no staying power.

❧ 25 ❧

Mom moved fast to start her new life. Within a week, she had transferred the few pieces of furniture she intended to keep over to her condo and had scrubbed and vacuumed the old house to its best advantage. The realtor made a few suggestions and then listed the house for sale. Another week and it was sold and Peter had packed up his meager belongings and moved to a modest apartment on the other side of town. In a moment of compassion Mom gave him the TV and the couch. Helping Mom with her move, I acquired Grandma Crenshaw's china, Great Grandma Worster's platform rocker, a box of pots, pans, and kitchen tools, a share of the nice linens, and an aching back. Mom's new place was bright with lots of windows, pale yellow paint, light tan carpet, and cream-colored tile in kitchen and bath. We parked Dad's car under the carport and I took her to the BMV for a beginner's permit and to the driving school for her first lesson. She confessed to a few nervous qualms but in the event, she soon recalled driving rules and former skills.

The Fake Force (nickname for the Anchron Fraud Task Force) met on a Thursday afternoon. I sat through a mind- and bottom-numbing series of reports on the investigation of the stock transfers but snapped sharply to attention when the floor was turned over to Detective Rodriguez. He summarized his findings in the Cash inquiries in a list of points.

1) The M.E. reported a fall or push had rendered Betty unconscious when her head struck the corner of the bureau. Subsequently and very soon thereafter, a bed pillow had been pressed over her face with sufficient force to crush her nose and lips, *vide* blood on the pillow. The cause of death was suffocation.

2) The M.E. set the time of death as midmorning on Sunday (the day before I found her body). There was evidence of recent, probably consensual, sexual activity. See Item 4, below.

3) Detectives determined the bedroom had been rifled, trinkets of little value and clothing tossed on the floor, two chairs and a bedside stand turned over. The false bottom of a jewelry box had been torn up apparently in a hunt for cash. Officers found an envelope taped to the back of the bureau and containing ten $100 bills. Forensics had failed to find fingerprints anywhere in the house.

4) The victim's bed had been slept in. Semen found on the sheet had been matched by DNA to her ex-husband, Officer Howell Broward, who admitted to a "conjugal visit" on Saturday before her death. Among bedclothes tumbled on the bed was a fuzzy slipper matching the one found on the victim's foot, and a picture frame. The picture frame was distinctively painted red, white, and blue; Officer Broward identified it as an item formerly hanging intact in Mrs.

Broward's restaurant and said it was not visible during his visit. The frame was empty, except for scraps of photo print paper dangling from the inner edge; the major part of the photo presumed to have been in the frame had not been recovered. Forensics had found four threads of fabric believed to be from antique painter's canvas, caught on a nail on the inner edge of the frame.

5) None of the outside or inside house doors was closed or locked, including the back door leading to the alley.

6) Testimony of Mrs. Emily Houlihan, a semi-invalid observing the victim's house from the opposite side of the street, identified Officer Broward visiting on Saturday between 2 and 4 P.M. She was away on Sunday but identified a young woman arriving on Monday morning in the middle of Dr. Phil's program (N.B. 10 to 11 A.M.), staying only 10 or 15 minutes, and driving off in a hurry. The car was blue and had two doors but Mrs. Houlihan couldn't specify make or model. (N.B. the driver was later identified as Ms. Cosima Elaine Crenshaw.)

7) Ms. Crenshaw reported the crime anonymously at 11:20 A.M. Monday but came forward three days later with a full story (N.B. See Interrogation report, particularly for description of a painting she believed had been removed from the frame found at the scene.)

The members of the Fake Force seemed to be hearing this sequence of evidence of murder for the first time. Clearly they began to entertain the notion that their financial criminals were possibly murderers. I valued Rodriguez's presentation for its logical flow. Rodriguez went on to relate steps taken to deal with Al Grover and Dolly Mead. Al had paid what he intended to be a flying visit to Dolly's studio last week, only to be taken with her into protective custody. The two of them were very little fish as far as the execution of the fraud went but their testimony would be critical to prosecution of the guilty Anchron executives and Betty's murder made them vulnerable. Both were scared enough to cooperate with Fake Force when offered immunity for their testimony. Ben's boss, head of the task force, reported the connection of the Anchron people with their couriers was fully supported by a collection of sightings, interviews, and phone records. Arrests of the Anchron executives were imminent.[*]

As the Fake Force meeting broke up, I looked at Ben and said,

"Well, that clears the air a bit, but I still don't know where that painting is, who took it, or who killed Betty Cash. Rodriguez will get Betty's killer sooner or later, and I'll be glad for it, but I still have a problem, don't I?"

"You sure do, but now that Fake Force is concluding its work, I can break free from time to time and spend my talents and time with you and incidentally to your quest. How does that grab you?"

I said it grabbed me just fine. And it gave me an idea to grab Ben and plant a big grateful kiss on him. Surprisingly he kissed back, thereby giving me a whole new group of ideas to wrestle with.

---

[*] Indeed, the 6 o'clock TV news featured Hamilton Waller and William Hacker in their Armani suits, flanked with lawyers similarly garbed by Armani, being escorted to a police car parked at the door of the Anchron skyscraper. The network anchors were already cranking up sidebars to explore all the ramifications of the arrests.

❧ 26 ❧

Ben had said he had looked into Wicker's move but I wanted to see for myself. So the next day I drove over to Wicker's old address. The building I remembered was a pile of rubble. A yellow behemoth on caterpillar treads, dangling a big bucket on the boom of a crane, clawed at heaps of broken brick and concrete and dropped its loads into a short line of dump trucks parked at the ready. A sign on a corner of a cleared area announced redevelopment by Slater Properties, **"prestige accommodations for discerning tenants"** and a phone number. I was looking at gentrification in progress. A straggle of storefronts on the opposite side of the street courageously faced the demolition operations. Gregor's Menswear offered overalls and steel-toed work boots for the blue collar crowd. Every chair in Lila's Ladies Hair and Beauty Spa was occupied. A dusty display window crowded with what looked like junk was flagged with a whitewash come-on, "Repair parts—obsolete applyances—this week Specal on Whirlpool." The door of a narrow but well-kept façade under a sign proclaiming Maisie's Café welcomed customers Monday through Saturday, 9 A.M.

to 9 P.M. On a hunch, I dropped in to find a dozen pedestal stools at a long bar and Maisie herself presiding over the grill and coffee pots behind it. I was a lone customer, the place was immaculate, and an inviting odor of cooked onions pervaded the air. I ordered a burger and coffee, relying on appearances that Maisie was above purveying food poisoning with her wares.

"I hope you don't have to fire up the grill just for me," I said. "Seems like you're not very busy today."

Maisie replied with an easy smile as she put water and cutlery at my place.

"Oh, no trouble. Lunch crowd is gone, supper crowd ain't due till five or so. How about some pie with that burger? Fresh-baked this morning, apple or pecan. The apple is special good with a gob of ice cream."

I fell for her salesmanship and we chatted pleasantly about the changes in the neighborhood as I ate.

"Ought to be good for us," Maisie said. "Been pretty dead around here for the last two years, but condos goin' in will be good for Lila's and my business. Gregor'll do good while construction crews is around. People like you don't come in often. You a reporter or somethin'?"

"No, I was looking up a man who has, or had, an office at an address across the street." I flashed Wicker's business card. "He must have been a customer of yours. Would you happen to know where he moved to?"

"Johnny, yeah, nice guy. He was a regular. But he didn't tell me anything. Just picked up and went one day. Him and Higgy used to talk a lot, about the teams mostly. Hey, Higgy!" she yelled suddenly at the half-open door of a back room.

A large hairy fellow in a very dirty apron appeared in the doorway.

"How in bloody hell am I supposed to get this room cleaned up with you hollerin' at me all the time? Whaddya want?"

"Did you ever hear Johnny Wicker say anything about where he was goin' when the building got torn down? This lady is tryin' to look him up."

"Naw. He never said nothin' but I wouldn't be surprised if he went Altamor way. He had a sister over there. What's this woman want with him?" Higgy was experiencing an attack of suspicion. "He didn't have to pay alimony any more, his ex got married again."

"The Mr. Wicker I'm looking for is a private investigator and I may have a case for him. Any idea what his sister's name might be? She may be able to put me on to him."

"Naw, he never said nothin' about her 'cept she lived in Altamor." Losing interest in the conversation, Higgy returned to his chores.

Maisie poured me another cup of coffee. I had exhausted the information to be had in this establishment, and the others seemed unlikely sources, so I paid my tab and left

Back at my office, I found an ornate invitation to a gallery showing, featuring wine and cheese and a hitherto unknown artist. Since Giovane had gone missing again, I decided to renew my contacts in the art scene. Gallery goers often gossiped more than they purchased. I dressed up in heels and little black sheath for the evening, planning on drifting about, eavesdropping, and chatting up prospects. As I entered, Lisa Galloway, my friend and the owner, erupted in a scream of delight and descended on me in a flurry of jangling beads and flowered floating voile. She dragged me over to stand under the main chandelier, where her heavily hennaed hair glowed in a brilliance I found blinding but not unexpected. Lisa had always been like that; flamboyance was her stock in trade, aside from paintings.

She grabbed a meek little fellow in a threadbare tweed jacket, introduced him as Karol Kostas, FIND of the DECADE. Kostas had sad eyes and a drooping black mustache. I made a mental assessment that his art had better be outstanding, since his person wasn't memorable enough to win a following. After a few polite words I captured a flute of cheap champagne and started a stroll from picture to picture. I was standing in front of an eye and nose meticulously rendered in mauve and black when an elderly man in a wheelchair came up beside me. I recognized him as Laurence Keefer, the art critic for the daily newspaper.

"What in God's name are you doing here? I hope not buying," he burst out.

"Lisa's a friend. I'm certainly not buying. The Museum patrons I try to please would upchuck on their shoes if any of these went on the walls."

"Glad to hear that good taste and appreciation for real art are not dead. This guy should advertise his work as 'School of Warhol in Purple and Black.' Might give it some distinction! What are you working on back at the shop?"

We chatted on for a few minutes about the Bernardino oils currently on loan, then Keefer suggested I check Jannie Wall's gallery, where I might find some reasonably priced, quite nice late Renaissance sketches. A software billionaire was cleaning out his art collection, putting the profits in a classic car collection.

"Any little Rembrandts?" I tried to keep my voice disinterested.

"No, none of the big names. But had you heard that Jannie's nephew, Caspar the forger, got out of jail in February? A visit henceforth to view

Jannie's offerings of Old Masters will provide considerable food for thought, don't you think? Caspar was one of the best at his craft and I doubt he's lost the skill or the will during his incarceration. Jannie tries to be honest but that wife of his spends his money like there's no tomorrow and Jannie might … well, 'nough said."

Indeed, enough said. News of an accomplished forger on the loose was worth noting. Caspar Wall had been convicted for forging 18th century miniatures similar to the Cosway I had just bought for the museum, but he was noted for superb technique and abilities in a wide variety of genres. Until he was caught out on the miniatures, his primary employment was with a major movie studio as a copyist of masterpieces for set decoration. I resolved to look very closely at any new piece I saw offered as a bargain or as a loan to the museum. After a few more conversations on this and that, none of them laudatory of poor Karol Kostas's pieces, I bade Lisa goodbye and headed home.

❧ 27 ❧

Over the next several days, I visited a number of galleries and collections within convenient driving distance. A lot more gossip came my way, most of it unremarkable, but several curators whispered word of Caspar Wall. Those who didn't were those I suspected weren't above shopping one of Caspar's copies to a gullible buyer. Touting the copy up front as "not authenticated but quite decorative; at this price you can't go wrong" made a small profit without risk of penalty. I learned no useful information on my rounds and by Friday morning, I was sitting at my desk riffling through a stack of sale catalogs. When my phone rang, I hoped to hear Ben's voice but it was Detective Rodriguez asking me to stop in at Altamor P.D. A new development, he said, perhaps I could help. I arranged to be there at 1 P.M. and tried Ben's number to ask whether he was available to join me and he was.

Rodriguez welcomed Ben; the more the merrier he said although his face belied any promise of a cheerful session. He sat us down opposite his desk. A large brown grocery bag marked with yesterday's date and "A.P.D. 06-32" sat on the blotter.

"Our officers responded yesterday to a citizen's report of a burned out car in a ravine a few miles from town. The fire had apparently occurred some time ago. A body, severely burned, was recovered from the vehicle. The license plates were still legible and the car was registered to John R. Wicker who we determined is licensed as a private investigator in Durgan County."

Frozen in shock I swallowed hard against the nausea that threatened to overwhelm me. Ben reached for my hand and held it while Rodriguez went on.

"I called Ms. Crenshaw because she had indicated at the Fake Force meeting that John Wicker had been in touch with Mrs. Broward. I have alerted Mr. Conrad's superiors to the possibility the dead man is John Wicker and have been asked to keep them informed of all findings in our investigation. DNA testing is in progress and we have initiated a search for a relative of John Wicker."

I spoke haltingly, "I learned last week that John Wicker has a sister who lives in Altamor. Will that help?"

"Yes, thank you." Rodriguez made a note, then reached into the brown bag and drew out several photographs and a plastic bag containing what appeared to be a charred block of wood.

"The state police are helping us in this investigation; their forensics people have gone over the ruins of the car and determined use of an accelerant. The M.E. has not completed the autopsy. The body is not entirely unrecognizable and the M.E. tells us the face of the victim is a match to the photograph on file with the license application in Durgan County. We are proceeding on the assumption that the body is that of John R. Wicker. I intend to spare you the photographs. No wallet was found on the body or in the car, but this," he pushed the plastic bag containing the black thing across his desk to me, "was found under the driver's seat. Ms. Crenshaw, have you any idea of what it is?"

I put out my hand toward the bag but withdrew it with a shudder before I replied.

"When I interviewed Mr. Wicker in his office, I asked for the address and phone number of a daughter of Adrian Cash. He looked it up in a rather thick leather-bound book, maybe four by six inches. This thing might have been about that size and shape before it suffered so much from heat and flames. I suspected at the time that it held current case notes as well as names and addresses. He took it from an inside coat pocket and returned it to the same place."

"We hoped you could tell us more about it. We have not found a residence or an office for Mr. Wicker since he moved from the now demolished building. We want to examine his office equipment and files. Can you tell us exactly when he last contacted you?"

"The day Betty Broward is said to be killed. But I didn't talk to him. He left a message with my landlady but she had an accident and couldn't pass on the word for another week. Her version of his message was 'Fifteen hundred cash and it's yours' and 'Tell her Jay Double U, she'll know.' I figured Jay Double U was his initials, J.W. He was a secretive kind of person. I thought I had told you about this at the Fake Force meeting."

Rodriguez sighed, " Yes, you did. I wish we could know what is hidden inside that hunk of coal."

"We can, we can." I rushed to say. "It's not easy but there are people, we have one on the Museum staff, who work with historical documents found damaged by fire, water, or insects. They can, for instance, open pages to disclose legible material."

Ben finally entered the conversation. "Detective, I've heard they do miracles at Treasury with damaged paper currency and bonds. We could ask my boss to get Treasury to work on this but the job would get low priority and it would be months before you learned anything. Why couldn't you let the Museum restorer work on it?"

Rodriguez was willing to entertain that option but hurried off to get permissions from his chief and the district attorney. That charred chunk of mystery was, after all, evidence found at the scene of a crime. After a lot of paper work, labeling, photography, signatures, and telephone calls, I left Altamor P.D. with the black thing in the plastic bag in another brown paper grocery bag. Missy Boonstra, the specialist at the Museum, pounced on it gleefully.

"Been a long dry spell since I had a challenge like this," she said stripping on surgical gloves. "But tell 'em it won't be an overnight job. Picking apart fused pages of a book like this and photographing them one at a time, front and back, before they crumble is painstaking work."

"Can you keep me posted as you go? There are two murders in play and even snippets of information may help in their solutions."

"Sure, get Jonesy to loan me a darkroom assistant and I can give you day-by-day's worths of pages as I get 'em shot. How about that?"

I made the arrangements and resigned myself to patience. For the next week, my day began with a review of photos of salvaged pages and repeated disappointment. Missy had to begin in the center of the book where the legible dates were several weeks before Wicker's call to the Puckett House. I politely suggested Missy progress toward the back of the book where I suspected the juicy bits were to be found. She counseled patience, patience, patience and I tried to be philosophical.

≥ 28 ≤

While I was sweating out the project at the Museum, Ben was
following developments with the Fake Force. Hacker and Waller on
the advice of their high-priced lawyers were keeping their mouths
shut, having pled not guilty. Evidence in hand though incomplete
was nevertheless convincing enough to get an indictment and to cause
remand of Hacker and Waller without bail. But what was emerging
from new evidence was a carefully orchestrated plot, initiated on a
small scale three years ago and maturing full scale in recent months.
Treasury agents had located and questioned several counterfeiters
considered capable of copying the complex etching on genuine shares.
Two of them admitted contact two or three years back by a businessman
with a mysterious agenda and offering almost irresistibly profitable
remuneration. At the time they were under close surveillance by T-men
and both swore on their mother's graves they had turned him down.
Pressed to describe the businessman or to identify him from a photo
lineup, one said he had only spoken to the man on the phone, the
other admitted conversing with him in person. The guy who actually

met the man described what he judged was a disguise using cosmetics, hair pieces, and thrift shop clothing and shoes; he recognized none of the subjects in the photo lineup. Another lead the agents had turned up was a purchase of high-quality watermarked paper almost identical to that used to print genuine shares. The anonymous purchaser ordered by phone, picked up the paper stock in person, and paid with cash. The man was not recognized in a photo lineup, but was described as a "hairy fella with bad B.O." This transaction had occurred in January of the current year.

The flow of money to Caribbean banks had started as a trickle probably in trial runs and remained undetected by corporate audits for two years. It had become a flood in the months the couriers were carrying fake shares to the African companies selected to be defrauded. The payments made by these companies were directed to a special account at Anchron, supposedly dedicated to executive pensions; the account was controlled by Hamilton Waller and audited in-house by William Hacker. The computer trails for Waller's and Hacker's criminal activities were so intricate and involved that Fake Force accountants were chewing their nails in frustration as they untangled them. They had, however, succeeded well enough to win the current indictments.

Ben told me all this over pastrami and sauerkraut on rye at our favorite deli. I then told him about Caspar Wall now out of jail after serving a three year sentence.

"He's good at whatever he tries. I never heard of him counterfeiting money or financial paper, but he would probably welcome the challenge to etch plates, maybe even to print the product."

"Well, the fake shares we've recovered are very well executed, both the etching and the printing. Whoever did them was good at his craft. Where is this Wall guy? We don't have him on any of our watch lists."

"His uncle is Jannie Wall, a somewhat shady gallery owner. He may know, but maybe wouldn't be willing to admit it. He might have Caspar hidden away in a loft or deserted warehouse somewhere churning out copies of Old Masters. Maybe a parole officer has an address for him, assuming he's on parole."

"We'll go to work on that. How's Missy coming with Wicker's pocket book?

I groaned. "Slow, but the dates on the pages she's recovered are approaching the time of Betty's murder. Would you like to see the pictures of what she has so far?"

Ben said yes, but balked at the number of prints there were to review. He had several appointments on his schedule and wouldn't be free for another couple of days. We arranged to meet then and go over the prints together on the assumption that two heads would be better than one to assess obscure clues.

Mom called one day and asked me to dinner at her new home. I arrived with a pot of orange and gold chrysanthemums. She blushed with pleasure.

"No one has brought me flowers since I was a girl. I love these. Don't they go well with my décor?"

And indeed they did. She had purchased a sectional sofa in brown faux suede and a glass-topped coffee table. Graceful lamps stood on handsome end tables and several excellent flower prints matted on grass cloth hung on the wall.

"I'm rather proud of my finds for this living room," she said shyly. "I got the sofa and lamps at a second hand store and the tables at garage sales. Everything very inexpensive. The prints are calendar pictures I got at a garage sale and matted and framed myself. I've made a couple of new friends my age living in this building and they have been very complimentary."

She looked expectantly at me for the approval I was only too willing to give. Dinner was a roast of pork with sweet potatoes and baked apples. She informed me proudly she was attending lectures on nutrition and personal care, a program offered free at the community center in the condo complex. She was enjoying life and new experiences; she had lost some weight, her skin was fresh, and her color was healthy. I admired her and everything she was doing and she bridled with delight when I complimented her. I felt obliged to ask after Peter but so great was her bliss, she was able to talk about him without a shadow of emotion.

"When I first moved here, he phoned every day to bemoan his fate. I finally told him I didn't want to hear from him but once a week. When he asked me if I had cable TV and could he come visit, I said NO!" She laughed and pointed to her 9-inch color TV. "See that. I told him my TV was a one-person set and didn't run for anybody but me. He still moans and groans on his weekly phone call; I listen for 5 minutes then I tell him I've got other things to do and I hang up. And I don't feel one darn bit guilty!"

We had an enjoyable evening lingering over coffee. I found it almost unbelievable that Mom had things to talk about: recipes, clothes, PBS programs, new acquaintances, even old grievances. One thing she shared gave me considerable food for thought.

"I know," she said, "estrangement from your father was painful for you. I always hoped the two of you would make up but I guess it was not to be. Although I was sure you were Ed's child, he never was. We were separated for a year and I got pregnant as soon as we got back together. Ed blamed me for the separation; he wouldn't believe that I had not had men friends while we were apart. He never could accept you fully and it made him mad if I favored you." Tears shone in her eyes and her voice broke. "It was something I could never explain to you till now. I'm sorry."

There was nothing I could say except to reassure her that I didn't blame her and my grudge against Dad had died with him. That wasn't entirely true but I was trying to believe it enough to make it so. I thanked her for a lovely evening and said I hoped she would ask me back whenever she felt like it.

❧ 29 ❧

The next morning I sat down to my collection of prints of pages rescued from Wicker's pocketbook. Missy had often ordered multiple exposures or enlargements of some pages in order to bring out detail; consequently, twenty recovered pages had ballooned into 70 or 80 prints. Most of those pages appeared to list coded cases in play and hours devoted to each of them. I squared the stack neatly before I added the previous day's harvest, just one page which dated from the week before Betty's murder. It was relatively well preserved. Although the outside edges of the page were badly charred, four entries had survived. Selecting the prints that retained the most and the most legible information, I could make out several important items, among them digits I recognized for the Puckett House phone number. Another entry was a street name, West Ridge something followed by several digits of a phone number; I guessed it was Betty's address and number. The words "alley off Merritt" and the numeral "9" appeared beneath it. A barely legible line held the initials C.W. and a complete telephone number. Below that was another partially legible number, probably the area code for Altamor and the three digits of an exchange.

I sat back in my chair to await Ben's arrival. I was sure the most recent page was the most valuable recovery but I figured it would be unwise not to review all of them. While I waited, I verified the Altamor area code and exchanges from the telephone book I was keeping in my office these days. I also searched the map of local area codes; the C.W. number had to be located in the Enterprise Industrial Park on Highway 20 in a neighboring county. I waved my finds triumphantly at Ben when he came. He proposed following up these new clues before reviewing the remainder of the prints.

"Hmmm, C.W.? Who do we know with those initials? Not Waller, his first name is Hamilton. Wall? Caspar Wall? Why would Wicker have his phone number? I'll get on to the phone company to get the subscriber to that number, and if we're lucky and it's a wire line, an address. I'll also try to get the geography of that exchange in the Altamor area code. Are you sure the number with the West Ridge entry is Betty's?"

"What's left of it matches the number Wicker gave me when I was hunting her. What do you suppose 'alley off Merritt' means? The numeral may be a time for an appointment."

"Let's try a 'what if' scenario. What if Betty and Wicker were planning to meet at her house but Betty or he didn't want old lady Houlihan to see him coming or going? I think we need a street map of Altamor."

Reference this time to the street map in Altamor's phone book found that Merritt Avenue crossed West Ridge Canyon Road a block south of Betty's house. Aha! Our what if scenario seemed feasible. And it raised another what if. What if Wicker had come to negotiate a buy from Betty, killed her intentionally or accidentally, and rummaged her possessions to find and tear Giovane from his frame? Might have an observer spotted him in the alley the day Betty was killed? What if Betty was already dead when Wicker got in the house and he took it as an opportunity to hunt and reclaim Giovane? Wicker knew the frame and contents of the Object. Why then would he have called me in the afternoon of the day in which Betty Cash died and leave his cryptic message with Mrs. Puckett if he knew Betty Cash was already dead? Was he trying to sucker me into discovering her body? If he hadn't killed Betty, who had?

Ben and I discussed possibilities for a while without developing any more "what ifs" and then Ben left to follow up on the phone clues. He was going to drop in to see Rodriquez, to give him a copy of the most recent print recovered from Wicker's pocketbook, and tactfully to inquire how thoroughly householders abutting on the alley had been interviewed. In an attack of guilt for so much neglect of my Museum responsibilities I tackled some woefully belated paperwork and tried not to think about dead people for the rest of the day. When I got home that evening, I found an invitation Zulu had taped to my door. Spaghetti and meatballs at 6? Of course I accepted and we ate and chatted, trading trivia and house gossip. I asked about Mrs. Puckett. Zulu said Amos Puckett said her rehab was going to be long and arduous and when she could walk again, he was taking her into his home. He had offered Zulu the job of house manager until she graduated and she had accepted. Easy money, she said with a grin.

"Oh," she said suddenly, rummaging in her pocket, "I found something you should have. We got a past due notice from the gas company and I was looking back through Mrs. P's papers when I ran across this message form on a spindle. It's for you, or it was."

The pink form was filled out for ZC, dated 5 P.M. Saturday, "Mr. Double called, message about 1500 cash." But Mrs. Puckett had told me that message came on *Sunday* afternoon just before she fell.

"Were there any message slips for Sunday?" I asked.

No, Zulu said that slip was the only one on the spindle. By golly, I thought, Mrs. Puckett's memory was off by almost 24 hours! But no wonder she misremembered the day. She had told me about the message more than a week after she took it and after major surgery and a lot of pain medication. Although I didn't know what good it did me, I now knew Betty wasn't dead when Wicker left his message.

The next morning, Detective Rodriguez called to ask if he could come to see me. Sure, I said and he arrived so promptly I decided he had called on his cell phone from the Museum parking lot. He rather sheepishly related that he had spent most of yesterday re-interviewing people in the neighborhood for a passerby observed on a Sunday morning in the alley off Merritt. As he pulled a tiny tape recorder from his pocket he was muttering something about slipshod work by patrol officers.

"Listen to this," he said, turning it on.

A woman's strangled voice coughed a few unintelligible words then continued.

"That morning, me and the mister went to seven o'clock Mass. When we got home...."

She interrupted herself in a fit of coughing and Rodriguez explained with one word, emphysema. Having caught her breath she went on,

"Anyway, I fixed us a nice little brunch and it was such a pretty day, we took it out on a tray to the table on the patio in the back yard. We was eating it and I said to my husband, 'There's somebody late for church taking a shortcut through the alley, must be going over to Merritt Street Methodist.' And my husband says, 'Well, you'd think them Protestants could get up early enough to get to church on time.' The bells was just ringing 11."

Rodriguez's voice asked her to look at a photo. But she said,

"We couldn't see him all that good, just noticed he was dressed nice, suit and tie, carryin' a briefcase. He was goin' toward Merritt, like I said."

The next segment Rodriguez played was all in Spanish, his voice slow and his words carefully enunciated, a woman's rapid and angry. He had taped it at a convenience store on the corner of Merritt and West Ridge Canyon Drive. He translated for me.

"I showed her a picture of Wicker and she told me she hadn't seen anybody like that. Then I asked if she had seen a dark gray VW sometime on that Sunday morning. That's when she got mad. Business on Sunday morning was mostly people coming in for the papers, a gallon of milk, or snacks for the afternoon football. Her parking lot isn't very big and it makes her mad when people park in it without coming in and buying. She wrote a big note in real mean words and put it on the VW's windshield. The note said if he didn't get out of there, she was going to call the police. She even wrote down the license number on a scrap of register tape and stuck it in the change drawer. Then she got busy and when she looked again, the car was gone. She managed to unearth the paper for me and the license was Wicker's."

"That puts Wicker almost surely in the neighborhood about the time Betty died, doesn't it?" I mused. "And I have a bit of news for you. His message to me was left on *Saturday* at 5 P.M., not Sunday afternoon as Mrs. Puckett told me. Here's the note. As you can see the time of the call was actually 18 hours or so before the time the M.E. said Betty Cash died. "

Rodriguez carefully updated his notes, and rose to go. Then he turned with a parting bit of news for me.

"By the way, we found Wicker's sister, Cathryn Wicker Johansen, a widow 62 years old; she wholesales arts and crafts supplies from a warehouse in the Enterprise Industrial Park. The telephone number from Wicker's notebook is the warehouse phone. DNA matches confirm it was Wicker in the burned out car, dead from a gunshot to the base of his brain before the fire."

A now familiar wave of nausea flowed over me. Hearing how Wicker died was almost worse than finding Betty dead. Too many deaths. Why Wicker? Why Betty? Where was Giovane? Was he smiling maliciously at my agonizing? I tried to work the rest of the day but my mind kept turning the questions over and over, a poignant distraction from my work.

❧ 30 ❧

By midafternoon I was fed up with trying to work. My curiosity was burning hot. I wanted to *DO* something, and the something I decided to do was look up Mrs. Johansen's place of business. The coincidence of an arts and crafts supply store with my lost painting was irresistible motivation. So I drove out on Highway 20 and into Enterprise Industrial Park. I found JOHANSEN ARTS AND CRAFTS SUPPLY on Cotton Street next to a feed store and across from a commercial laundry. It was a large, high-roofed building. An office suite was located in the building behind a large plate glass window. On the window, a tasteful sign read OPEN M-F 8-5. Inside were two women, one at a computer, the other at the counter leafing through a bulky ledger. I pulled into the feed store parking lot so I could survey the area without attracting attention. A cement block barrier separated the parking lot from a drive that led to a sizeable paved area behind the Johansen building. There bales and crates were being unloaded from an 18-wheeler backed up to a wide door.

I glanced at my watch and at the sky. It was 4:30 and a long time until November twilight would set in. So I drove to the service district out on the highway and browsed in a Dollar General Store and a Kroger until 6, then patronized Wendy's for a malt, French fries, and a burger which I ate as slowly as I could. I had made up my mind I would try to get in that back door once it was dark and I cooked up a plan. Returning to the Dollar Store I bought a heavy screw driver, and a flashlight and batteries. I cased Highway 20 in both its north and south directions. Killing time until dark was the hardest job I had had in a very long time. It was more boring than my experience with a useless stakeout. But at last, the cars that passed me were turning on their headlights.

I drove back to the feed store which was now dark and entered its parking lot, pulling my car behind a panel delivery truck seemingly parked for the night. I assembled the flashlight and put it in my purse, congratulating myself that I had that morning chosen my most capacious one for the day. The business office in the front of Johansen's was dark and I sidled down the drive toward the rear of the building. The wide freight door in the back of the building was standing open; the semi's trailer still stood in front of it, its doors wide open. Hugging the outside of the building I crept close enough to peep past the trailer. Male voices seemed to come from far inside a cavernous space that was full of boxes and bales stacked in blocks 10 and 20 feet square. Narrow aisles led between the blocks of merchandise. A few dim lights glowed in the dark emptiness of the high ceiling. Since no one was in sight I risked slipping inside around the trailer and ducking between the nearest blocks. My heart leaped into my throat when I heard men's voices and footsteps coming down the main aisle but the footsteps passed my hiding place without incident. Then the trailer's doors slammed shut and two men got in the truck cab and slammed its doors. The truck drove off in a roar and gust of diesel fumes. Now I had a clear view of a wall of concrete blocks forming a room in the back corner of the building and a door standing open in the wall.

I relaxed but then had to resist an impulse to sneeze. It was a good thing I succeeded. As I peered from my vantage point a third man came down the main aisle to a switch box beside the big door. The lights in the main space went out. The man then reached inside the door of the concrete wall, flipped off another switch, and banged the door closed. In the dark, I couldn't make out the man's features but his shadowy outline grabbed a lever on the freight door and started it closing. The man skipped under and through before it fully closed. And there I was—closed IN.

I drew a deep breath. I was IN and that's where I wanted to be but I was nevertheless acutely uncomfortable. I hadn't committed breaking and entering but I had certainly entered without an invitation. I squatted on my heels and listened for a long time. All I heard was the patter of tiny feet, mouse feet I devoutly hoped, and the creaks and groans of a metal building adjusting to night time temperature. At last I turned on my flashlight and swung the beam around the space in front of my hiding place. A neat stack of office furniture was piled in a corner of the outside wall. I was shocked to recognize the battered desk and gray file cabinets I had once seen in John Wicker's office in the now-demolished building. I tiptoed over to verify my first impression and was further astounded to see a dusty brief case lying on the desk top. Was this *the* brief case? The one he carried the Sunday morning when he was last seen? Then I began to think logically. Why wouldn't he beg storage space from his sister when he was obliged to move? Where else would he keep his brief case when he didn't carry it?

What really captured my interest, however, were the concrete walls and door of that room standing in the opposite corner. Cautiously, soundlessly, I left the shelter of the block of boxes stamped Product Of China and approached its door. I froze at the sound of a vehicle revving its engine in a nearby parking area. I stopped and held my breath until the sound died away, then went to the door and, with my shirt tail in my hand, grasped the knob and turned. It wasn't locked. Luck was with me. Inside, I became aware of large bare windows high up on the outside north wall. Just like an artist's studio, I thought. I was careful to keep the beam of my torch well below them as I swung it around the room. More amazement, this *was* an artist's studio. Several pieces of finished art leaned against the wall. Two easels stood next to a table littered with tubes of paint, a palette, and a can of mineral spirits. A spectrum of carefully cleaned brushes was laid out on a pad of newspaper. Generous daubs of colorful paint splattered the floor and a high stool. Everything about the place screamed "Artist at work." I was ready to bet my next year's salary that C.W. at this phone number was Caspar Wall. The work on the easels was covered with protective cloth, a sign of work in progress, oil a-drying. I flipped up the cloth on one of the paintings and my heart nearly stopped. Giovane's teasing glance looked back at me. I hastily flicked off the cover of the other painting; again Giovane's face but this one unfinished. Caspar was copying the real Rembrandt and doing an excellent job. I wasted no time going after Wicker's briefcase and bringing it into the studio. I had no doubt that Giovane had been in that briefcase when Wicker was seen carrying it down the alley from Betty's house.

And that's where I put Giovane now. I yearned for a better light so I could verify the original painting on the spot but swallowed my impatience. This was no place to linger. I packed up the copy as well, tacky paint notwithstanding. A quick look around at the items lined up against the wall reassured me that they were of no interest to me. That was when I noticed a wall and door in the back of the room. I opened it and in a quick glance noted an absence of art and the presence of a cot with rumpled blankets. Caspar must sleep over sometimes. Stacked milk crates made a pantry for some canned fruit and several kinds of crackers. Then I heard the sound of a vehicle in the parking lot and made a dash for my hiding place behind the shipping crates. I managed to get the door shut and my flashlight off before I heard fumbling at the big door. When it went up, I saw Caspar Wall flip a switch and a flood of overhead light illuminate the space in front of the corner room door. Caspar walked up the main aisle toward the business suite and when I thought his back was turned I raced for that big opening and out into the parking lot, clutching the briefcase in a death grip. I tore over to the feed store lot, expecting every minute to hear a burglar alarm go off or at least Caspar bewailing his loss. But nothing, so I started up the car and drove as fast as prudence allowed to the highway and back to the Museum. I let myself in, waved at the patrolling guard, and went into Jonesy's office.

There I flung myself into a chair and practiced deep breathing. Fortunately, Jonesy's desk sported a box of Kleenex, because I had a good many tears of relief and tension, joy and triumph to mop up before I locked the office door and opened the briefcase. I was half afraid I would find ashes and pebbles, Santa's gifts to a sinful child, but no, there were the paintings. I carefully lifted out the copy and reverently removed the original. Now that I had a proper light and the magnifier that lived on Jonesy's blotter, I knew it was indeed the original Rembrandt. The craze marks in the paint that I remembered so clearly from the insurance company's photograph were all there and in all the right places. I flopped in a chair and practiced breathing control again. I was suddenly exhausted. The adrenaline rush had dissipated. It was all over but the shouting but I didn't have energy left for a chuckle, much less a shout. Moving like an automaton, I opened Jonesy's safe and installed my prizes. I twirled the tumblers, made a sticky note that said DO NOT OPEN UNTIL I AM HERE WITH YOU, and stuck the note on the door of the safe. Then I took the empty briefcase to my office, locked it up, and left for home. Ten strokes were ringing out from the campus bell tower.

❧ 31 ❧

I fell into bed, unwashed, in my underwear, too tired to put on a nightgown, and slept deeply. I woke at first light, my mind clear, my energies at full throttle. I took an unauthorized shower, dressed for the day, and called Ben. I could tell from the sleepy voice and grumpy tones I had waked him, but I comforted myself with a glance at the clock: 6:30 and time he was getting up.

"Meet me in Jonesy's office by 8 A.M. I've got big news," I caroled. He growled an "OK" and signed off with a decisive click.

I was 10 minutes early but Jonesy was already in, lounging in his big swivel chair with his feet on the desk. When I burst in, he waved in the direction of my note on the safe and asked,

"What is all this? Must be big. Let's get at it."

"Wait and see. Ben's on his way."

Ben arrived 10 minutes later, grumbling at traffic and the early hour. He was his usual well-groomed well-pressed self, shaven, although he had missed a patch on his left cheekbone. I found that endearing and greeted him fondly. The two men welcomed Susan carrying in a pot of fresh-brewed coffee. I locked the office door behind her exit and started hurriedly to twist the dials of the safe. When it opened, I pulled out the Rembrandt and propped it against the terminal of Jonesy's computer. The men stared open-mouthed.

"Is that what I think it is?" Jonesy half-shouted.

Ben said nothing but grabbed me and kissed me, on the mouth no less. Wriggling free, I pulled the copy from the safe and set it next to the original. Although the copy Giovane was unfinished, the face was fully developed. The fur on the red tippet was lined out but obviously in progress, as was the silky sheen of leather and velvet on the shoulder of the doublet. Now Jonesy and Ben were startled all over again. Jonesy peered through his magnifier at the original and the copy in turn, whistling his recognition and approval of the original.

"It's the real thing," he said, his voice awed. "How in heaven's name did you come by it?"

"I burgled it," I answered. "Sit down, you two, and be prepared to hear a tale of derring-do and luck."

My euphoria and ebullience led to some slight embellishment of my description of events and I basked in self-satisfaction for a story well told. But when I finished, I noticed serious disapproval on both Jonesy's and Ben's faces. They spoke at the same time, Jonesy saying, "Great work, but tricky. You could have been caught at any time. Foolhardiness is not part of your job description." And Ben scolding, "Didn't you stop to think? My God, woman, don't two murders raise a black cloud over the paint and canvas of these two pictures? You might have made a third victim if your luck had run out, and may yet."

I swallowed my disappointment; I had wanted to be praised and petted for my achievement and all these two guys could come up with was blame. I changed the subject. "Forget it. What are we going to do about this?"

Jonesy hastened to answer. "Hey, Leave me out of it. I don't choose to be one of *we*. You can keep these in my safe but I got nothing in anything beyond that. I'm not only chicken, I'm careful of my reputation in the world of art and education."

"Well," Ben drawled, "I guess I'm sticking with you. Let's put these things away in the safe, they're evidence after all, and then you and I should go to your office and re-examine the documentary evidence. Maybe we can come up with a convincing way to whitewash your foolishness when you talk to Rodriguez, as talk you must."

Wicker's dusty briefcase lay on my desk. Ben opened it and began going through its compartments. He came up with a pair of white cotton gloves, a small screwdriver, half-a-dozen pens and pencils, an empty notebook, and three paper clips. Then he noticed a small tag of displaced lining and pulling on it, disclosed a piece of paper from a yellow legal pad, folded small.

Ben unfolded it carefully, then said, "This is handwritten in pencil; it looks like the draft of a letter."

"Well, read it." I urged and Ben began.

"Dear Cath,

If anything happens to me and you find this, I want you to know I had nothing to do with that Cash woman's death. I had an appointment with her that day because she wanted me to negotiate with the Emmons woman to get more for that picture of her father. She offered me half of whatever I could get

151

and you know I haven't been too prosperous lately. But when I got there, she was dead, the place had been tossed but the picture was still hanging on the wall. I knew the Rembrandt was behind the photo and I pried it out. I didn't see why I couldn't reap some benefit from it. Emmons still had a reward out on it. But then I did some thinking and decided I could do even better. I knew I could sneak the painting to Mexico where some people I know could put it in the international pipeline for stolen art. Cap Wall was hanging out in your warehouse and he was an expert copyist. Why not return a copy to Emmons? She already had her insurance money, she wouldn't know it was a copy and wouldn't be about to insure it again. I could claim the glory and the reward and pay Cap generously and he wouldn't dare grass on me, seeing he had that counterfeiting job to conceal. I think I have a lead on Betty's killer but won't put it on paper. Too dangerous, you understand. You've been a good sister.

Love, J."

"Well, this explains some of the puzzles and poses others, doesn't it?" I said.

"Yes, and these gloves explain the absence of fingerprints in Betty's house. Wicker must have known of Wall's talents and career already. The letter seems to indicate he knew or suspected Wall as the counterfeiter of those fake shares. We can take this letter seriously, it's like a deathbed confession. Seems that Wicker recognized a crisis of conscience just long enough to conquer it and choose the dark side. Did he suspect Caspar Wall as the killer, do you think?"

"I've met Wall, not to know him, but enough to judge his temperament. I would think violence would be the farthest thing from his ken. He's small, wispy, effeminate, soft-voiced. Of course, even a pussy cat might turn into a tiger with the right provocation. I could imagine him worshipping the Giovane, rejoicing in its proximity while he copied it, but not killing for it."

Ben refolded the yellow paper and tucked it back in place in the briefcase. Closing the case, he said,

"We, take note I'm saying *we*, should head for Rodriguez without further ado."

Just then, Missy Boonstra's gofer appeared with yesterday's photos. We went through them hastily, noting only a telephone number we had not previously seen or guessed. We took the photo and briefcase with us to Altamor and Rodriguez's office. He was sitting at his desk clutching his temples when the duty officer ushered us in. He raised his head and exploded in a gust of discouragement.

"This damn case is driving me nuts. Every lead is turning into a dead end, even with the T-men helping!"

"Take heart," I soothed. "Maybe we have something in our latest batch of news that will get you off dead center. Here." And I put the briefcase down in front of him. When we left a hour later, Rodriguez's enthusiasm had been rekindled.

❧ 32 ❧

He had shared his strategy with us. Caspar Wall was new to him. Bringing him in for interrogation as well as getting a warrant for a thorough search of the Johansen warehouse became first orders of business. Ben concurred and would get his boss on the Fake Force to assign him to join the A.P.D. in their inquiries; particularly to search for plates and the press he suspected Wall had used to create the fake share paper. Also on the agenda was exhaustive questioning of Wacker and Haller to explore the hitherto unknown connection with Caspar Wall and perhaps John Wicker. As for my escapade, Rodriguez's reaction to my story of recovery of the Giovane was first anger at my foolhardiness and secondly intense interest in the letter hidden in the briefcase. The letter explained a great deal. By exonerating Wicker of Betty's murder, it gave a new focus on Howell Broward, Betty's ex-husband. He was known to have been perhaps the last one to see her alive and questioning him might well be profitable. The detective puzzled over the new phone number the restorer had found in the wreck of Wicker's notebook.

"I've seen it somewhere before. But I'll run a trace to be sure."

"And what am I to do with the paintings?" I asked. "I don't intend to turn them over to you although I can tell you they are absolutely safe and can be produced for inspection under strict conditions. I also don't intend to tell Agnes Emmons her Rembrandt has been recovered until the murders are cleared up. Have you any other suggestions?"

"Well, I would like to verify with my own eyes that they exist. Among the things I do not intend is charging you with unauthorized entrance to the Johansen warehouse. With that said, are you willing to arrange a viewing?"

"Of course." I said and we planned to meet at the Museum after Wall had been taken into custody. The meet did not occur for another two days. Wall had not returned to the warehouse and it was not until Mrs. Johansen learned of her brother's connection with Wicker that she was willing to tell Rodriguez where Wall was living. The warehouse had been searched from top to bottom and wall to wall but the only find was a few sheets of the special paper used to print the fake shares. When at last Caspar had been located and taken in for interrogation, Rodriguez invited me to observe through the one-way glass. Meanwhile Ben and his team were searching Wall's apartment and storage cage.

Caspar Wall was as I remembered him, thin blond hair drooping over a face as ill-defined as pudding, long flexible fingers, a pudgy body. His mien was submissive and evasive, his voice soft and well modulated. He reacted to every one of the interrogator's questions with an alarmed gasp, but his answers seemed (to me at least) to be truthful.

No, he didn't know Al Grover, Dolly Hack Mead, Betty Cash Hack Broward, Hamilton Waller, or William Hacker. Yes, he knew Johnny Wicker, he was Mrs. Johansen's brother. Did he know Wicker was dead, murdered? Read it in the paper. Too bad, Johnny was a nice guy, helped him find the studio in the warehouse, couldn't imagine why anyone would want to kill him. When the interrogator sprang the question "Did you kill him?" his composure broke into a squeal of fear and vigorous negation. Wringing his hands, he repeated over and over, "I couldn't kill anyone." When asked how and when he got the Rembrandt, he said Johnny had brought it to him at the warehouse; as to when, he couldn't quite say but maybe three weeks or a month ago. What did Wicker want him to do?

"Why, copy the Rembrandt, of course. It was such an honor, that gorgeous thing from the very hand of the Master. I get breathless just thinking about it. I've been working on the copy with a delicate touch, every day a little bit, to get it just right. At first Johnny came in to check on progress but after a couple of weeks he didn't come again. I told him I could get the picture perfectly but I had to use modern canvas and paints and any expert would detect that at once. He said it didn't matter. He'd get his money's worth out of the original one way or another. He promised me ten grand for the copy after he had pulled off his caper."

"Did he say how he had got the Rembrandt?"

"I asked and he said just plain luck and then he said I shouldn't worry, it wasn't stolen and nobody knew he had it. I believed him. Johnny was always straight with me, me and him and Cathryn grew up together on the same street on the south side of Altamor."'

The interrogator started over with did-you-know Al Grover, Dolly Hack, *et cetera;* this time Caspar was nervous and at Dolly's name, his hands clasped on the table involuntarily clenched. The next question was how did you know Dolly? He stumbled through an answer, the gist of which was he didn't know her but Johnny did, mentioned her name, said she had wealthy friends. By this time, Caspar was thoroughly shaken and when Ben arrived to join the interrogation and showed him his badge; Caspar immediately asked for a lawyer; and the interrogation came to an end. I came to a tentative conclusion that what really worried Caspar Wall were counterfeited Anchron shares.

Rodriguez led Wall away to be charged with illegal possession of a small bag of marijuana found at the studio. He couldn't be charged for copying a masterpiece; that was no crime until fraud entered the mix, and there was no evidence that Caspar had solicited a buyer on false pretenses. Rodriguez placed a new interrogation of Dolly Mead on his agenda and Ben and I walked out to have lunch at the kosher deli.

As we placed our trays on the table, Ben gave me a quirky look and said,

"It's like badminton, the shuttlecock batted from Rodriguez's side to Treasury's side and back. I sure as hell wish we could knock it down for good on my side."

"You know, Ben, I'm beginning to think Betty's and Wicker's murders have nothing to do with the Rembrandt or investigation of the fake shares. Everything we know about those murders seems so peripheral to the painting and the fraud. Are we and Rodriguez barking furiously down two of three rabbit holes when we should be barking down the one we have so far neglected?"

Ben gave me a sharp look over his pastrami on rye and swallowed his last bite.

"You may have something there, but what's left that looks like a neglected rabbit hole?

"Howell Broward, Betty's ex-husband. Why did they divorce, why does Howell make 'conjugal visits?' Where was Howell on the morning Wicker found Betty dead? Aren't those good questions? If you don't mind my mixing metaphors, might not two of three rabbit holes be red herrings?"

And we left it at that. Ben departed to follow up on Dolly Mead and I went back to Altamor P.D. for a look at some records. By now I was such a familiar face over there that no one gave me much trouble when I asked for things. I came away with notes on three domestic disputes in the past three years when Betty Broward had called the police to report beatings by Howell Broward. I also looked up Howell Broward in the graduating class pictures from the Police Academy. The image was small and not too clear but I could see Howell was a big man, probably 6 feet or more, 225 plus pounds. Over at the Hall of Records I discovered the divorce had been granted 18 months ago on grounds of physical abuse attested by hospital records and granted uncontested by Howell Broward. From his age, I worked backward to guess at the year he might have graduated Altamor's only high school. Checking yearbooks in the public library I found a very good photo of Howell and ample reports of athletic prowess. I took a copy of the photo, hoping that the years had not aged that face beyond recognition. I ran into the "Blue Wall" when I returned to A.P.D. and asked to see the duty roster for the weekend of Betty's murder and records of disciplinary action against Howell. I would have to invoke Rodriguez's help on that. He was away and not expected back until tomorrow so I resolved to be patient. I resorted to the phone book for Howell's address but his phone was either unlisted or unpublished. I decided to be patient back at the Museum. Jonesy might be pleased if I resumed earning my stipend from the Torgerson Foundation grant.

❧ 33 ❧

Ben called to warn me he planned dinner at a posh spot, shorthand for a suggestion to dress up. He picked me up at six. He had chosen The Abbey, a restaurant so upscale that the *maitre d'* recited the menu in plummy tones instead of handing it to us. The building was formerly a church; splashes of color danced over the white table linens, silver, and crystal as a brilliant sunset lighted stained glass windows. After we had chosen our fare—broiled grouper and baby carrots for me, steak and Portobello mushrooms for Ben—a *sommelier* appeared to suggest our wines. I opted for the house white, a Chardonnay, and Ben ordered a German beer I had never heard of. I wondered if our dinner foretold basic differences in life style. As long as we were lunching on pastrami with sauerkraut we had seemed to be on the same dietary wavelength. I squelched my qualms, however, and reveled in the great taste and aromas of my meal. Then....

"Oh, Lord, Ben. There's Agnes Emmons, over there at that corner table with the man in evening dress. Don't look. Oh, I mean don't let her see you looking. Dear God, don't let her see me."

"What are you worrying about? She is obviously vetting that rich, elderly gentleman for the position of third husband. She's so engrossed in patting his hand and feeling his knee that you aren't in any danger of being noticed. I'm just glad to see the notorious lady. So far, she's just been a name. Now there's a face and a bosom bedecked with diamonds to remember."

To distract my fear of encountering Agnes's gaze, I abruptly asked Ben,

"Why this fancy dinner and venue? What are we celebrating?"

"Can't you just enjoy?" he laughed and then went on to fill me in on the latest news of the Anchron case. Al and Dolly were boiling over with information, naming names and places of encounters with Waller and Hacker. The Fake Force search team had gone over the warehouse again and found the plates for the fake shares.

"Where in the world were they? I thought that first search was down to the bare bones."

"Well, it occurred to one of our bright young agents that the walls of Caspar's studio room didn't reach all the way to the roof, went only about 12 feet above floor level. So he climbed up and inspected the top of the walls and found a kind of coping beneath which in the farthest corner lay the front and back plates wrapped in canvas. When Wall was confronted with them, he caved. He fingered the print shop run by an old acquaintance with a shady reputation. He had used the press and printed the shares after regular business hours. The old friend denied any knowledge of Wall's activities."

"Does that complete the case against Hacker and Waller?"

Ben took a deep draft of beer before answering.

"Not quite. Caspar also fingered our old friend, the hairy man in thrift shop clothes, as his contact first with the proposition and a down payment of $10,000, a second time to view the plates and give him the special paper, and finally to pick up the printed shares and hand over a final payment of another $10,000.. The meetings were set up by mail and Caspar was ordered to burn the postcards after reading them. Which he did. Wall couldn't pick the hairy bloke out of a photo lineup but claims he could probably recognize the guy's voice. The Fake Force team is arranging an audio lineup tomorrow. Even if Wall can't pick out his contact, we can let Hacker and Waller think he did and break down one or both of them. That will wind up the Anchron fraud case. All over but the trial, that is."

"Why, Miss Crenshaw," Agnes Emmons's voice came over my left shoulder like a summons from Sinai. "What are you doing here and with such a handsome beau?"

She had seen me but now I did the graceful thing and introduced Ben as a good friend and consultant to the Museum. Agnes beamed at him, then turned around and introduced her octogenarian companion as her brother-in-law, Edward Emmons. A brief exchange of trivia and then the question I dreaded,

"Have you found my painting? I read where that detective I used once had been murdered too. I'm beginning to think that your search is cursed by untimely deaths of people who have handled it. I trust you will get back to work after your dessert. I can recommend the *crème brulée*. I hope to hear from you soon. It's time for results!"

I met her harsh tones with an ingratiating smile and an insincere promise to bring her up to date as soon as I had one more bit of information. She snorted and hustled out of the restaurant hauling her brother-in-law along by one arm. Ben chuckled,

"*Femme formidable*! Have you decided what and how and when to 'bring her up to date'?"

"Yes, when we know who murdered Betty and Wicker, I'll tell her everything. I'll even give Giovane back to her, provided he's not incommunicado somewhere in an evidence locker."

"What about dessert?" Ben interjected. "I'd prefer flan to *crème brulée.*"

So we had flan and he drove me home. His goodnight kiss at the door was promising, passionate, and prolonged. I went up to my apartment humming *Someday my prince will come,* not even caring that wasn't what Cinderella was singing as she came home from the ball.

❧ 34 ❧

It was the following Monday before I could get back to A.P.D. and Rodriguez. He met me with a big smile, no sign of a headache.

"Boy oh boy, it's great to have the Anchron stuff out of my hair. Hacker cracked, if you'll pardon the expression, and Treasury has its case all sewed up. Now I can concentrate on murders. What can I do for you?"

"Well, I'm trying to follow up on Howell Broward. I asked to see the duty roster for the weekend Betty Cash was killed and whatever records there were of disciplinary action. Got turned down. I learned Betty charged him as wife-beater to win her divorce and I found a photo so I could recognize him when I got close enough."

"Dammit, woman." Rodriguez exploded. "The next thing I'll hear is that you you're dead. Why don't you let me do my job? That'll give me peace of mind and time to think about Howell Broward. I've been following up on him myself. That new phone number from Wicker's notebook is Broward's cell phone. And he was off duty that weekend. And he has a record of repeated episodes of excessive force in making arrests.

163

I've suspended him and asked him to turn in his service revolver, but he's got a lawyer and the D.A. has asked me to be prudent as I proceed. Suspecting a man in blue in a small community like Altamor has its repercussions. But I've just got the warrant to search his apartment for two other guns registered to him. Now, are you satisfied?"

I apologized and then started a new fire storm by asking,

"When are you going to bring him in for questioning? Can I listen in?"

"Any time and NO. This is police business and I'm perfectly capable of carrying it out without your involvement. Thank you for your interest, Ms. Crenshaw, and you may go now."

"OK, OK," I said and stumbling over his waste basket, made a less than graceful exit from his office. I had to admit he was right.

I had a full agenda of projects back at the Museum and spent the rest of the day clearing my desk and planning the next exhibit of American primitives. I had to run down some Clementine Hunters and Charlie Refsums that were in private collections. I was interrupted when Susan stuck her head in my door saying Jonesy wanted me to stop by his office before I left. I found him with pencil sketches spread all over his desk. Clearly he was making plans for the Emmons Wing that he expected to wring out of Agnes when the Rembrandt was back in her hands. I laughed and warned him not to count his chickens before they were hatched. But he chuckled and asked whether I thought the wing should be added on the north face or south face of the current building. We tossed around a few more ideas until it was time to close up shop and go home. Most of the museum staff had vacated the parking lot by the time I walked out to my car. As I put the key in the door, a tall figure loomed up in the dark behind me and put a strong hand on my wrist. Just then the headlights of a departing vehicle lighted the face of the figure. It was Howell Broward. I froze in barely contained terror.

"Ms. Crenshaw, I been hearin' you're askin' questions about me back at the station. I want you to know I'd take it kindly if you'd quit that."

He transferred his grip from my wrist to my shoulder; it was like an iron clamp and I was acutely aware that it was getting closer to my throat. I had no doubt that he could strangle me or break my neck with that one hand before I could scream. I wondered if I could talk him out of whatever he intended to do to me.

"Mr. Broward, I mean *Officer* Broward, I don't know what you mean. My questions were about your ex-wife Betty. I was asking about a picture of her father that wasn't found in the house after her death. I wasn't asking about you."

Broward's grip tightened and I dragged out my tired old story of writing a magazine article about Adrian Cash. "Her father was a famous movie star, you surely knew that. She was very proud of him."

A patrol car came running smoothly and quietly along the line of parked cars. It stopped with its headlights directed at me and Broward. His grip relaxed and his hand dropped away. Then I saw Detective Rodriguez get out and approach us.

"Hello there, Howell. What are you doing here?"

"Nothin', nothin'. Just wanted to see the girl that been askin' questions about me."

"Well, you've seen her. Now get in my car and let's go back to the station. Are you carrying a gun?"

Broward grunted a negative and went peaceably to enter the patrol car. Rodriguez flipped me a salute and followed. The patrol car moved off and I began to breathe again. My knees had turned to water; thankfully a park bench nearby allowed me to recover. To recover further, I left the car in the lot and walked home. An icy wind was soughing in the leafless branches and fallen leaves swirled around my feet. I shivered, wondering at the close shave I had had, wondering what Howell Broward really intended when he accosted me, wondering if Rodriguez was trying to teach me a lesson by waiting to the last minute to end the confrontation. Whatever, it was over and the welcoming lights of the Puckett House promised warmth and quiet. I debated whether to call Ben but, in the event, he called me. His voice was tense with strain but he spoke calmly. Rodriguez had notified him he had found Broward in dangerous proximity to me and that he had taken Broward in for questioning.

"I'm coming over. I don't want to violate any house rules but I intend to come up to your apartment and … well, I don't know what I'm going to do then, but I'm coming. It'll take me an hour to get there. Be decent."

I had to laugh. He had some antiquated idea of sorority house prohibitions against men on the second floor of the house. I put the coffee pot on, dug out a package of Oreos, and arranged the cookies on a one of Grandmother Crenshaw's flowered plates. I couldn't find flowery cups on short notice so I put out my dime store mugs. Preparations for a social event complete, I flopped on the bed to wait and fell sound asleep. When the door burst open, Ben erupted through it, calling

"Are you all right? Did he hurt you? Why are you lying down? God, woman, that had to be close. I'm more worried now than when Rodriguez told me about it."

He flung himself down on the bed to gather me up in his arms and the rickety slats that supported the mattress promptly collapsed under us. I burst into laughter and he assumed I was hysterical. He scrambled up from the wreck of the bed and jumped to fill a mug of water. I was laughing so hard all I could do was push his hand away. He finally caught on and folding me in a warm embrace, joined in my laughter. After simple repairs on the bed, the rest of the evening was more social than I had expected but satisfying for all of that. We did discover a massive bruise on my shoulder when I undressed.

ॐ 35 ॐ

Ben left in the cold gray dawn and I snuggled under the covers again, savoring the warmth and comfort, lumpy mattress notwithstanding. I had come to the conclusion Ben and I had something going and I rejoiced in it. I began to entertain thoughts of a June wedding. If Agnes came through with that extra $100,000 for finding Giovane, we could even have a luxury honeymoon. Although perhaps I should claim less of her offer. After all that had happened, it would be like taking blood money. Maybe I would negotiate some lesser sum, I mulled over round figures on the sunny side of $50,000.

My musings were interrupted by Zulu tapping discreetly on the door. I leaped up, threw on my robe, and let her in.

"I waited a while. Didn't want to interrupt anything. There's a phone call for you, a policeman. He says you aren't answering your cell."

"Tell him, please, to hang up and I'll call him back in less than five minutes."

I needed time to put on something warmer than my robe, Puckett House drafts were legendary. Rodriguez, when I reached him, was in a high state of euphoria.

"Howell confessed to both murders. He couldn't wait to talk, his crimes have been preying on his mind. We've got him on tape spilling chapter and verse. A part of me is very sad that a brother in blue violated his oath to protect and serve, but another part is jubilant that it's over and he'll pay for it, probably with two consecutive life sentences."

I risked another scolding and ventured timidly, "Can I see the tape?"

He didn't scold but he didn't say yes either. "Wait until the arraignment. He insists he will plead guilty, against the advice of counsel, and he'll be obliged to describe his deeds in court before the judge accepts the plea. The legal term is 'allocution' and for Howell it may be a way to give himself some sort of absolution."

"Have you told Ben yet?" I asked.

"He must be sleeping in this morning; he's turned off his phone. As agitated as he was last night, I expected he'd want to know …. But maybe, he had other fish to fry. I'll be talking to you. Go back to bed. It's a good day to stay there, there's two inches of snow on the ground."

Showered and dressed in my heavy winter clothes, I walked over to the Commons for breakfast and the papers. I encountered Juan over there, wearing his finest; sitting at a table, on his third cup of coffee, imbibing courage for his orals scheduled for 10 A.M. As we talked I tried to soothe his nerves, telling him his thesis was so good it would be easy to defend. After all, had I not helped him to polish it? He managed a few weak smiles and went off still nervous. I promised him Zulu and I would treat with pizza and beer for the celebration supper.

Then I breathed a short prayer that his committee would be as kind as his major professor was mean.

I walked over to the Museum, wishing I had more substantial footgear, and spent 20 minutes drying my feet on the radiator in my office before opening the paper. I couldn't wait to tell Jonesy the latest on the murders, but he was still so wound up with his plans for the Emmons Wing that he barely paid attention. As I left his office, he called after me,

"What are you going to tell Agnes?"

I sighed and shrugged. I would have to confer with the D.A. and Rodriguez before I had an answer for that. Giovane now recovered was more of an albatross around my neck than a meritorious achievement. I was grateful that he had a safe refuge in Jonesy's safe but maybe it wouldn't last. I called the D.A.'s office first and made an appointment for 11 o'clock.

The D.A. was a distinguished gentleman, gray-haired, a golfer's tan, a firm handshake.

"I'll be very glad to hear the story of the painting. It's been lurking in the background of all these important investigations and now we learn it may not have been central to any of them. Sit down and begin."

I told him everything from the moment Agnes Emmons made her proposition to the moment I put it in Jonesy's safe and spun the dials. It made a long story but he listened carefully to all of it, only asking an occasional question.

I ended my story with a question, "Now what do I do?"

"If there's no doubt the painting you were charged with finding is indeed owned by Mrs. Emmons, I see no impediment to your returning it to her. I must stipulate that the court will have an interest in it and

Mrs. Emmons will be required to allow its introduction in evidence should that become necessary to the prosecutions of Howell Broward and the Anchron malefactors. Let me come over to the Museum and see the thing and then with your permission, I will contact Mrs. Emmons and her lawyers to arrange its return."

I breathed a long sigh of relief. I had dreaded facing Agnes Emmons but with a D.A. running interference I thought I could do it with a clear conscience.

∽ 36 ∽

Lest my reader think it was all over but the shouting, I hasten to relate the final act.

I attended court the day Howell Broward pled guilty to manslaughter in the death of his ex-wife and first degree murder in the death of John Wicker. Standing very straight, shoulders braced, he made his confession in a careful monotone; I had to listen hard to catch everything he said. But the gist was that after his conjugal visit to Betty Saturday afternoon, he went out drinking. He returned by the back door after dark, after parking his personal car two blocks away, and enjoyed conjugality for the rest of the night. Waking on Sunday morning, he and Betty argued. She bragged about the money she made in her travels as a courier. When he wanted her to share, she berated him for lack of ambition, said if he amounted to anything he'd get promoted, make more money, and be able to pay his bills. She kept pointing to her father's picture where it hung on the wall and going on how handsome and debonair and successful he had been. Goaded beyond patience, Howell aimed a haymaker at her but she ducked and fell against the bureau. Howell thought he'd killed her but decided to make sure and pressed the pillow over her face. He made a cursory but unsuccessful search through her stuff, hoping to find her stash, then he left and went on about his life. He grew confident he had gotten away with Betty's death when A.P.D. questioned and released him, but he found it difficult to sleep and eat. He still loved Betty and was sorry she was dead....

Then John Wicker started to follow him around and ask questions; in one of their conversations Wicker insinuated he knew Howell had killed Betty. Finally Howell put a five gallon can of gasoline in his car, lured Wicker out to a meeting on a country road, threatened him with his service revolver, forced him down on his knees, and shot him in the back of the head. With Wicker in the trunk he drove Wicker's car to the ravine where it was found, put the body in the driver's seat, and torched it. He displayed no remorse; for him killing Wicker was an act of self-defense. He was sorry for Betty's death but not for Wicker's. As he fell silent, he stood with his big body slumping and head bowed. He straightened to hear the judge pronounce sentence. For a moment as I deplored the deeds he admitted, I grieved for the way he had ruined his life.

The Anchron prosecution proceeded about as fast as molasses flows at the Arctic Circle. The government's case was very strong, thoroughly substantiated and documented, but Waller's and Hacker's lawyers were smart and capable and found innumerable means to delay the process. Ben said, however,

"Never fear, they'll get their just deserts."

He spent a great deal of time out of town, mostly in the Caribbean islands following the money trail and in Africa following the trail of the counterfeit shares. He predicted that the Anchron mess would not be resolved for another two to three years. When he came home for a weekend now and then, he was usually so tired a date ended almost as soon as it began. I invested in a new mattress and box springs for our mutual comfort.

Caspar Wall went back to jail, 15 to 20 years for counterfeiting, his plates nevertheless praised for their consummate artistry before being swallowed up in the vaults of the Treasury Department for safekeeping. He was allowed canvas and paint and was said to be turning out elegant portraits of the turnkeys. Cathryn Wicker Johansen was cleared of complicity in Caspar's activities.

Giovane was in the main vault of the Museum while Agnes and Jonesy pored over prospective designs for the Emmons Wing. Agnes and her lawyers had worked out a deal with the insurance company; her donation of Giovane and two million dollars to the Museum made up for the two million dollars the insurance company had paid her when they declared the painting irrecoverable. The day after the D.A. had met with her and her lawyers, I received one of her inimitable summonses on cream-laid notepaper.

Dear Ms. Crenshaw,

I shall be at home at 4 P.M. on Tuesday next and will receive you then. We have business to clear up.

Very truly yours,

Agnes Cathcart DeWitt Emmons

Not knowing what to expect, I put on courage in the guise of my new suede jacket and tailor-made tweed slacks. I needn't have worried. Agnes presided over the tea tray without a single snide comment.

"You have my thanks," she said, "for recovering the Rembrandt. If you had not, it might have vanished into the underworld of lost masterpieces. Now it will be a gift to the ages. However, I hope you are not expecting me to live up to my original offer. I will not reclaim the $25,000 advance. But I wish to remind you I do not have the Rembrandt in my possession as I expected when I set you on your search. It now belongs to the Museum. Quite a gift, don't you think? A two million dollar painting and another two million to build a wing, all coming out of my pocket."

"You said yourself the Rembrandt is a gift to the ages. To have your name attached to it should be a great satisfaction to you. I must remind you that I did work hard and took considerable risks to locate and reclaim it. However, I would be willing to negotiate a smaller reward than your original one of $100,000."

My voice was firm although my innards quivered at my impertinence. Agnes responded quickly, "You are living up to my original estimation of you, honest and ethical but not soft. How much smaller?"

"Make me an offer," I retorted.

I could imagine the wheels turning in Agnes's brain. I was reminded of a joke I had heard. Do you know why rich people have so much money? They begrudge spending it. Agnes was thinking of the least amount that would pacify me but not make her look chintzy.

"How about another $25,000?" she said finally.

"How about fifty?" I countered.

175

She laughed and poured us another cup of tea. In the ensuing silence, she said,

"Done. You're no patsy. My check will be in your mailbox tomorrow."

And it was. After that whenever we met in the halls of the Museum she threw me a snappy salute with her hello.

EPILOGUE

The evening after Howell Broward's trial ended and after staff had cleared out at the Museum, I sat in my office trying to recuperate from a hectic week of mounting and shepherding a new exhibit. Jonesy had decided that a display of fashions from the 20s would liven up the spring season. He had wangled the loan of the English Department's collection of F Scott Fitzgerald first editions, and I was commissioned to make an interesting meld out of literature and costumery. I did not enjoy the job. Despite enclosing the suits, dresses, shoes, and hats in glass cases, the smell of mothballs and mold leaked out to overwhelm air conditioning turned up full blast. Comments in the visitors' book were lukewarm at best and downright nasty at worst. One woman wrote, "What in hell does this have to do with fine art?" It was unsigned but I suspected Agnes Cathcart DeWitt Emmons's acid touch. In the end Jonesy had finally had to admit the only intriguing part of the show were the period jewelry pieces. He was philosophical. "You did your best but let's admit it. You win some and lose some."

As I leaned back wearily in my desk chair, my gaze fell on a photograph I had pinned on my bulletin board. I had asked for and received a copy of the insurance company's photo of the Rembrandt. I pinned it up and looked at it often to remind myself that the hunt for Giovane had ended. Giovane's smile was still arresting, still teasing, but no longer malicious. His image hadn't changed; my vision had. In accepting the challenge to find him, I had become my own woman, cut my ties with my family and found them again. I had met a spectrum of interesting personalities and attitudes as I explored their relationships with Adrian Cash. I hadn't learned much about Adrian and what I had learned was not admirable, but he was in a way the thread that strung my search for Giovane together. I had seen death in the person of poor Betty Cash, but neither I nor Giovane had to take responsibility for it. The death of my father had given my mother back to me and relieved me of the anger I had always felt for him and my brother. I had met and captured the love of my life, providing Ben agreed. I gave the photo one last look as I turned out the lights and closed the door. "Thank you, Giovane," I said, "for everything."

Printed in the United States
by Baker & Taylor Publisher Services